W9-ANY-195

"Extraordinary! This novel is a kind of *Mrs. Bridge* but set in a stylish, hellish New Jersey, and this *Mrs. Bridge* is about youth, not middle age, and the ironies are subtle, violent, terrifying and beautiful. Rick Moody writes with meticulous originality. I feel like going out in the street and whooping. Such splendor!"
— John Hawkes

"An eloquently written debut."
— *Publishers Weekly* (starred review)

Winner of Pushcart's Tenth Annual Editors' Book Award, here is a rare novel of uncompromising vision and beauty set in Haledon, New Jersey, one springtime at the end of the American Century.

Haledon is a suburb in eclipse, located near Paterson, with declining industry and enterprise. The working class isn't working, the middle class is moving out. On the hills above the Middle Atlantic sprawl, the kids are looking for something to do.

Among them: Alice Smail, one-time guitar player and unemployed short order cook; Dennis Francis, painter and plumber; Max Crick, dealer in controlled substances; and Nails Pennebaker, night watchman.

Garden State is a stark novel about the lyricism of real life, the beauty of responsibility, the refusal to face either — and what happens after.

RICK MOODY'S work has appeared in *The Paris Review, Grand Street,* and elsewhere. This is his first novel. He lives in New York City. His next novel is *The Ice Storm* (Little, Brown. 1994).

GARDEN

STATE

RICK

MOODY

GARDEN

STATE

A NOVEL

PUSHCART

PUSHCART PRESS

Wainscott, New York

WINNER OF THE TENTH ANNUAL
EDITORS' BOOK AWARD

Sponsoring editors for the Editors' Book award are Simon Michael Bessie, James Charlton, Peter Davison, Jonathan Galassi, David Godine, Daniel Halpern, James Laughlin, Seymour Lawrence, Starling Lawrence, Robie Macauley, Joyce Carol Oates, Nan A. Talese, Faith Sale, Ted Solotaroff, Pat Strachan, Thomas Wallace. Nominating editor for this novel: Caroline Sutton.

Distributed by W.W. Norton & Co.

Cover photos by Rick Moody
Cover design by Cynthia Krupat
Author photo by Meredith Moody

and all in the back room at 46th Street

Without whom: Miriam Kuznets, Neil Olson,

Eric Ashworth, Helen Schulman, Betsy Lerner,

Allen Peacock, Barbara Heller, the Feelies,

Laura Browder, Lorimer F. Burns, Susan Schorr,

Susanna Sonnenberg, Kennedy Fraser, Melora Wolff,

J. K. Eugenides, Donald Antrim, Barbara Jones,

Dan Barden, David Means, Cynthia Krupat,

Bill Henderson, Caroline Sutton, Julie Rose,

all Saxons, Davises, and Moodys.

THE

MONTH

OF

APRIL

1 / Drizzle coated Haledon, N.J., with a sad, ruinous sheen. First of April and Alice the rhythm guitarist for Critical Ma$$ was idle, killing time at her mother's house as she had killed it in high school and after. Nick, the drummer, was lost to community college—it was two weeks ago now—and this loss proved mortal for the band. But attendance at Ben Dover's, bar of choice for locals (overlooking the Dern River, in the dilapidated manufacturing district of that municipality), registered no absence, no change in the scenery. The barflies blundered in as previously.

Rail lines marked the perimeters of Haledon, this isosceles triangle in the flat Eastern part of the Garden State. Freight trains ran through it like blood cells, carrying unpronounceable compounds and toxins. They rumbled past the accidents at crossing gates, past the crime scenes and late-night waste burials.

Hills rose above town, to the north and west. Where Alice sat now was among the affluent homeowners on the cliffs of the town's perimeter. The vast expanses of the New Jersey plains were visible from there—to the east, Paterson, Fleece, Mahwah; to the south, Jersey City, Tyre, the Oranges. The city proper sprawled down below the heights, and along one side of it the trains skirted an unclaimed territory, trains so long they seemed still to inhabit the past in the present moment, trains that completed a statewide circuit of manufacturing needs.

Then, on the hills, for a moment, the sun burst from the clouds over luxurious properties, each acre with its vocabulary of flora: oak, maple, ash, pine, willow, forsythia, rhododendron. Lawns dappled in sunlight. Everything in numerical proportions.

For two weeks now, the elements had wrought blankness upon the signs Alice had pasted onto telephone poles, post office boxes, and anywhere there were interdictions against signs:

DRUMMER WANTED.

ORIGINAL MATERIAL.

CALL ALICE.

And beneath, the number.

They were steadily eroded, these signs, by the dismal spring rain—only some industrial toxin could explain the relentlessness of it—and the results resembled ancient parchment. The signs were consigned now to some dead letter office of posted bills with the legions of unelected political candidates and lost pets. They were as unreadable as hieroglyphs.

There wouldn't be another drummer, though Alice had songs she could play with a new band. Dover's was a wasteland to her now. Those old chords, the easy chords, those open vowels she had sung, those thrashing fast, fast numbers, those images of glory, those theories of everything. They were gone for now.

She was twenty-three, jobless, living at home, roaming her mother's house, where there was a sound system in every room, where there was video tape, audio tape, large screen television, a cellular phone. Of her father's departure, last December, this was what remained. He lived across town now, in a newly renovated apartment. He sold units in condominium complexes.

When Alice's mother turned up, bearing groceries, she found her daughter swinging her electric guitar in dangerous arcs. Scuffs marred the paint job in the corridor, the old yellowing paint job.

She asked Alice to be careful.

Alice grunted.

Her mother passed into the kitchen, and set the groceries on the old flimsy card table there. Alice followed sullenly.

"You'll never guess what happened," Mrs. Smail said.

Alice teased through the bag of groceries on the folding chair, rummaging to the bottom.

"Well, I was speaking to Ruthie Francis at the store and she told me her boy, Lane, you know, had moved back into town. Out of the blue. He went into the city and now he's home again. A perfectly good job and now he's home."

Mrs. Smail held a bag of potato chips before her. She stared blankly at them.

Alice said nothing.

"Things were troubling him. This is what his mother told me."

Alice watched the replenishment of shelves. She moved the bag of groceries and settled into the chair with an exaggerated sensuousness.

"So?" she said.

"You knew him didn't you?" said Evelyn.

"I used to see him around some. He knew Max down the street, not that that made him friendly with me or anything."

"Oh?"

"They were big in the chess club."

Mrs. Smail rested. She surveyed the neighborhood through a small window by the refrigerator.

"Now, Dennis—"

"Of course," Mrs. Smail said. "Well, I just thought it was interesting that"—outside a crow tumbled from a tree to yank some prey from the surface of the lawn—"there he is and here you are. Both—"

"Nice," Alice swiped at the salt and pepper shakers on the table, overturning them as she rose. She gave the folding chair a parting shove.

Evelyn Smail sat down herself. She rifled the bag at her feet. Again, amid fears of product tampering, she found she had bought an open package of aspirin. Once her daughter had dared her, in the supermarket, to drink from a gallon of water without a cap, and while she pretended the suggestion was ludicrous, she had gone back to seize the bottle while Alice was in another aisle. She had drunk greedily from it. The effect was bracing.

In the meantime, in the living room, Alice was isolated in her own daydreams. Two weeks earlier she had driven out over the Jersey plains trying to sort out Nick's retirement from the band. Amid the desolate marshes outside Newark, she had passed an overturned car, nose down by the side of the road. The Pulaski Skyway overhead. Spectral chemical spills stagnating in the bay. Clouds stampeding across the plains. The car was on fire, and Alice pulled over to watch. Beside her, the traffic passed at illegal speeds. Stiff gales swept over the marsh and the smouldering smoke and flame spun upwards in helixes. No stranded driver made his way along the shoulder kicking the gravel and swearing. The authorities did not appear. Just Alice and the abandoned car.

It reminded her of Mike Maas. A guy who had actually set himself on fire back when they were all younger. It was next to I-81, in a marsh. Poured unleaded octane on himself, tindered it, and then stumbled up onto the breakdown lane. It was the most famous rubbernecking delay in Garden State history. It was the most famous self-immolation. Still, the memory was just a memory. It didn't make a difference now. What would, now, not Scarlett the bass player for Critical Ma$$, the only one in the band that she liked? She watched the car burn. She thought about insurance fraud. She thought about the future. She was back in the living room; she was out on the road.

Light faded. The first of April had come to Haledon without insects and the pleasure of this was ominous. The rain had rained itself out. Cloud formations overhead now would be visible soon in Paterson, Ho-Ho-Kus, and further, Bolt, Fleece, the Empire State, like some grand bit of news scrolling across the television set. Mrs. Smail opened the large porch windows. Birds tittered. The warmth was thick and humid. She sat in a wicker chair and sipped her drink.

Upstairs the ragged noise from Alice's stereo, and the sound of her electric guitar threading a needle through a repetitious passage sounded lonely to Mrs. Smail. But there was a lot that sounded this way to her. The freight train, for example, that was just then passing on one side of town or the other or the other.

Through her daughter's stripped white hair, black

lipstick, torn jeans, dog collars, and steel-toed boots, Evelyn Smail continued to recollect a voluptuously soft girl child—thick strawberry-blond curls, baby pudge. No matter the indiscretions Alice committed, the opinions she advanced, to her mother the past still held sway. Or it had until recently. Or maybe it too had been steadily eroded. During her tenure as a counselor to abused children, for example, Mrs. Smail had come into a set of anatomical dolls. She had little use for their totemic erections and cavernous orifices, but they were so repugnant to her she had trouble returning them to the proper authorities. When they disappeared from the house one day, she knew right away where they had gone.

Later, of course, Alice had them at school. Alice had taken a small, outcast, runt of a boy into his rest room, and there, with the pair of dolls, she had instructed him in the ritual of copulation.

Was that all? Mrs. Smail had asked herself on the way to the authorities. Wasn't there any more to it than that? There was no persuasive laying-on-of-hands. There was no perversion. What was the problem? The two of them were caught, simply, with the dolls. Her hands gripping his gripping the dolls.

It was the first of many such incidents. Alice was immersed, after, in lengthy consultations with the psychologists at school, professionals in the field. Whatever disordered her thinking, however, eluded them. With devotion that yielded only sometimes, Mrs. Smail had persisted in the belief that some sweetness would emerge in her daughter in her early twenties. But she was confronted only with unemployment, a steady stream of unwholesome boyfriends, and rock and roll. For Lent, Mrs. Smail had promised herself, Alice could stay. For Lent she had promised not to bring up the matter of her moving out. That left six days.

A figure parted the shrubbery outside, and appeared before Mrs. Smail full length in the screen window. His hands cupped his mouth as he prepared to speak. Of his face, she could only make out the sunglasses.

"It's me," he said. "It's me Dennis."

Some youthful method of entry, a modern version of the tree-scampering and gutter pipe gymnastics of her own generation. Well, she asked him to come around the proper way and to fix her another drink. He could have one himself if he liked.

Soon Dennis sat in a wicker chair across from Mrs. Smail, one leg crossed carefully over the other. He seemed to feel no need to speak. Mrs. Smail watched him watching her. His hair was a hopeless tangle of cowlicks. He had a soul patch whiskering a half inch under his lower lip. He wore paint-stained jeans and carried a wrench in the pocket. He wore a torn white tee shirt.

Upstairs a record came to a halt.

Mrs. Smail remarked, as she had before, about Dennis' mother, Ruthie. Not gifted at conversation, especially with the young, it was one of the topics she fell back upon.

Dennis reminded her that Ruthie was his stepmother, that his real mother lived in Paramus. But Mrs. Smail thought ahead through these biographical details. She was thinking about the question she had meant to ask all along. About his brother about—

"Stepbrother," Dennis said.

There was an awkward pause, and then he was rising to leave. Those requisite moments spent with the parents of a date had come to their end. He was not flushed. He simply rose. Mrs. Smail remained.

Upstairs, record sleeves scattered like fallen petals. Drawn blinds cast the room in a pall. Alice was seated on the floor in the middle of the room, beside the sculpture which had occupied her peripherally for several years: a folding chair pitched on its side with stainless steel cutlery wrapped in loops and corkscrews around its struts and legs. Ashtray emptyings, lingerie, condoms, handcuffs, plastic dinosaurs and army infantrymen were strewn in the negative spaces or glued or taped into carefully selected locations.

Alice played her guitar unplugged now, clicking her tongue in time with a repetitive pair of chords. Dennis watched.

He had been coming around the Smail's place at nighttime for months, since about the time her father had moved out. It was to sleep together, really, or so he thought, and though they did, there were long stretches between encounters. With him it was a need, a persistent rash of need, but Alice had strange rules governing these things. Dennis was helpless to produce the language that produced the act. There was a language, but he hadn't learned its idioms. There were some indicators with Alice, and sometimes he was able to kiss her, to entwine a finger in her belt loop: when a train was passing, when Alice was wearing blue, when there were sirens, when there was no moon, when amphetamines were spilled and rolling on the carpet. But this kind of stuff was by no means certain. Even though this afternoon Alice was wearing blue: a torn denim skirt.

Dennis cleared some of the laundry from the floor and settled down beside her.

"Talked with your ma downstairs," he said.

She propped her guitar against the practice amp.

"Play any tricks today?" she said. "Fool anyone?"

"Fooled your ma maybe."

They were older than having to wait for Mrs. Smail to leave, although the burdensome waiting of adolescence had created possibilities that were gone now. Adulthood proved the poverty of imagination. No more squeezing into a closet or lying under a bed. Alice had found she wanted less but could get away with more. When Dennis launched himself onto her she felt— even though strictly speaking she felt nothing—as though the day made sense. She rolled him over. They slid to the floor. They laughed. Alice managed to throw a record on the turntable while he was working on her with his tongue. She took the time to think of the right record and didn't get hotheaded about it. Dennis tried to get a pair of panties around her head and then around her mouth. Once he had fought his way in, Alice fought back and disarmed him by tying off his hands with the legs of his jeans. Well, maybe he wanted his hands tied off. It was messy and awkward and it took a long time. Fucking was nothing that would change the world. After, they lay aside and waited out the slowing of pulses.

Downstairs, Mrs. Smail fixed another drink. At the bar, she selected from crystal that seemed inappropriately to remain in the house like a layer of dust, after so many of her things were gone.

She had kept the European performance automobile. That was hers. It had comforted her, until the revelation that the model was being recalled for starting by itself. A woman in the next town had run over her husband. If only Mrs. Smail could run over her husband. If only she would find him standing out in the driveway one day.

And she had all the silver. She used silver to spoon applesauce from the jar, to slice artificial cheeses, to serve take-out Chinese food, because silver was all she had now. And she had the house. Still, how little genuinely pleased her—it used to be the quality of New Jersey sunsets which made her heart sputter with gladness, and the spires of churches that dotted the hills above Haledon, and the black squirrels that lived here and nowhere else.

On nights like this she sometimes called her ex-husband to shout accusations (and she was thinking here not only of possessions he had taken). But tonight she had settled on a drive. Yes, a drive. It was cooler now, and the nights had begun to seem longer. The evening light of April seemed to detail the reveries of arsonists. The sunset smouldered over the foothills.

From the bottom of the stairs, Mrs. Smail called up to her daughter: "I'll be back soon. I'm just going for a little drive."

No reply expected above the din of the record player, none came.

Sex smelled to Alice like industrial byproducts. It must have involved equally potent chemicals, those that were both organic and dangerous. She sometimes hallucinated the smell of spermicidal jelly in the course of the day. There was its faint redolence in guacamole or in fresh ink. In words, too, sex leaked outwards—laughter and fright, with their silent consonants, always reminded her of *diaphragm*. Try to ignore a thing like sex, and it turned up in everything.

"So tell me about this stepbrother of yours," Alice said. She was lying on her back, her head clumped in the middle of a tangle of laundry on the floor. She pulled her black leotard back up around her hips.

"Which one?" Dennis said.

"There's others besides Lane?"

"Nah."

"Well, so what's the problem?"

Dennis tossed a lightly smouldering cigarette butt onto the overturned chair in the enter of the room.

"No problem," he said.

"Oh, yeah. Then why would he come back here? Not like for rural luxury or anything. I thought the point was to get out and stay out."

Dennis looked at the record sleeve on the floor. He studied it without answering. It was that album with the Radon Belt map on it. An infrared map highlighting areas of prevalence.

Alice asked if Dennis wanted potato chips or if he wanted a shower. They could shower together. Dennis wanted chips. The corridors were all but pitch dark. They bumped into one another, into banisters and open packing boxes. At the top of the stairs, Dennis waited. She grabbed him around the wrists. They were both laughing.

"Why won't you tell me?"

"What?" he said.

"About him."

"Because it's nothing. I don't know. I guess he's homesick or something."

"Homesick for here?"

"Well, so now he'll get better I guess. Unless now he's homesick everywhere."

Mrs. Smail's absence went unnoticed. Between Alice and her mother, sometimes days passed in this way. She and Dennis arrived in the pantry suddenly, as though the house had grown huge with night and misdirected them into new wings and expanses. They found the potato chips in the cupboard and passed the bag back and forth, carrying the bag with them as they toured the unfurnished vaults of the first floor, passing from the kitchen to the living room to the porch.

Something was leaking from between Alice's legs.

"We should go out for beer," she said.

In the dining room, Alice grazed the rheostat on one wall and a chandelier splashed light across the dust pinwheeling at their feet.

"Take the van?"

"Yeah," Alice said.

"We could go to the city," Dennis said. But he suggested this often. "Or we could just go to Dover's."

"Yeah," Alice said, "Dover's."

And soon they were slamming shut the doors on Dennis' van, parked out in front of the Smail residence. Out on the streets, their headlights picked up the remains of Alice's leaflets on mailboxes and telephone poles.

Every car in the parking lot at Dover's was missing a headlight. The bar itself had two personalities. There were the working guys from the rubber plant just across the river who, at sundown, were avoiding home, tying one on, looking for a matinee. And then around ten o'clock, the first wave of youth. Both crowds were regulars.

Once the night crowd had been a high school crowd, but the legal drinking age had been inching upwards. Now college I.D.'s abounded (the state school i.d.'s). The Haledon High graduating classes that had been grandfathered over the years had ruled Dover's by majority and could remove a punk with industrial laminations at the least provocation. The tastes of this class prevailed and time seemed to have halted ever since.

Along the rear wall, the bands occupied ten square feet of proscenium. There was no room to dance, but no one danced here anyway. There were no grinding thrusts on stage, no complicated unisons. There was no dancing in the aisles around the tables. The public address system at Dover's was left over from years past, from square dances or public auctions. Sound emerged from it as muddy and menacing as a highway skid. The guitars, played through the miked amps rather than through the P.A., were inaudible to the bands. So they turned up louder still. Only a narrow sonic corridor cleaved its way through the acoustic silt of Dover's, and this accounted for the lyrical obscurity of Haledon bands, and the hegemony there of *Metal*.

When Alice and Dennis got there, D'Onofrio was on. They came once a month from Paramus in a gray Econoline van. Alice had despised them from the first, their triteness—I want you bad, let's have a good time, don't treat me mean—their inability to get their bass player to learn all the chord changes, their stolen hubcaps, their platform soles.

She and Dennis drank at the corner table, close enough to one another that they didn't have to squirm to shout in one another's ears. While Alice watched the band, Dennis kissed the back of her neck. She waved him off. He was grateful at the drop of a hat. The evening was tedious but he was grateful anyway. Alice remembered that she had sworn she would never be here again, and here she was.

Then, Louis, the lead guitarist from Critical Ma$$ strode in. He was wearing his pink leather trousers and a black satin shirt opened to the waist, a leather dog collar, a smudge of rouge. Alice sank lower in her chair. For a while L.G. hoisted sweet drinks at the bar, but in the time Alice forgot about him, in the time she stopped scrutinizing his every movement, L.G. was moving toward the stage. Soon he hopped up there with D'Onofrio and slung a spare guitar over himself. The band dove into the opening eight of Devil on the Devil Train. Even Alice felt her pulse register the first downbeat. It was just one of those songs. Some sounds were like pacemakers to the lounge lizards of Haledon, the heart-lung machines of an age—piercing harmonies that didn't quite lock, solos as fast as automatic weapons, melodies like the roar of industry. It got in the blood.

Alice felt lower than she had in years. They were into the rave-up Devil Train chorus, and that was right when she realized that nothing had come of the years since high school and that nothing would come of the years ahead. Nothing had ever been worse than this, not her parents splitting up, not Mike Maas' death, no global horrors—none of that made a difference. Maybe it was the drinks.

All attention turned to the final solo. L.G. pounding on the neck of the guitar, on the last couple of frets. The song ground to a lurching halt, as always, and all stood. Applause, applause. Sure enough, next would be West of Network. It was the star turn in a starless town.

"I don't know what I'm going to do," Alice said, holding Dennis' head close to her mouth, her cheek against a clump of uncombed locks. "I swear, Dennis, I don't know."

Dennis waited for her to stop and then pointed to his ear, shook his head.

After a second volley of appreciation, the song ended, and L.G. unslung the spare guitar and tossed it, as though this were a major arena, to a guy on the floor, and then he leaped from the proscenium into the crowd. At Alice's table, he turned the third stool around and sat backwards in it, his palms draped across the top like some fabulous jewelry. Blandly, they said hello.

"Listen," L.G. said, "I'm going to audition for this band, Slaughterhouse."

Alice folded her arms.

"Things were fucked up anyway. And with Nick gone—"

"Do what you want," Alice said.

"Slaughterhouse has a manager. They're professional. They're at like a professional level. And like we—"

She was leaning forward now, pointing. "I can't believe you fall for that. You're gonna be playing marching tunes."

L.G. betrayed nothing.

"You're a real bitch sometimes," he said.

Alice smiled. The din of action at the bar, D'Onofrio beginning to load their equipment, these receded for Alice as she stared at him. "Do whatever the fuck you want. Doesn't mean anything in the long run."

He smirked. With upturned palms, he rose.

"Well, listen," he said. "No hard feelings, the way I see it. I'm having a party on Saturday, a party with music. Hope you guys can come."

"Rather be run over by a train," Alice said.

Just then the bartender dropped an entire load of beer mugs, fresh from thirty seconds immersion in some dangerous cleaning agent. Conversation came to a halt as L.G. headed for the door. Then the bar noise resumed.

Alice and Dennis stayed as the crowd turned over for the next band. Hardcore kids with mohawks and jaundiced faces unpacked secondhand instruments. An opaqueness had descended over the evening and Alice felt awash in hot passions that she could not speak of. Rage was the one thing she could put her finger on, but there was more to this than just rage. After a couple of numbers at blistering tempos, Alice decided maybe sex *would* help. She grabbed Dennis and held him to her. She grabbed the collar of his tee shirt, stretched it all out. In that arrangement, they stumbled out.

Flummoxed, he woke again in his room, still not recognizing it, not feeling himself to be named as he was, Lane, not feeling himself to be son or stepson or stepbrother, beloved of each, not feeling himself removed from the barely furnished cave he had formerly struggled to pay for, not feeling himself to be himself. How had he come here? The color pink was superimposed over everything; the sensation of nausea and of being constantly late for an appointment, these were fixed in his awakeness now.

He was in retirement. It was coming back to him.

Now the flowered wallpaper in his bedroom was not flowered at all, but covered instead with the double helixes of genetic information. His sudden ability to read these ideograms didn't surprise him. The blinking red light in each pattern, the gene for his madness which had waited in abeyance all through childhood, stood out in the patterns he saw. So this was him now.

While lying there in bed, he waited for details to return, as if his life were immersed in a photographic developing solution. All was elusive at first. He knew he had called his mother, after weeks of avoiding her, after weeks of ignoring what was sitting right in front of him—his ruined self—and he remembered that the explanation was like pulled teeth. Please come and get me, he had said at last.

And now he was drugged, sleeping sixteen hours a day. More to come.

Alice recalled the parting kiss. Dennis gone off with the first rude barbs of sunlight to snake some lines somewhere. For union wage. But before he had gone he had whispered something in her ear. Advice? And then he had kissed her. The particulars were hazy.

A needle of hurt ran from the base of her neck through sinew, muscle, bone, especially through her brain, and pierced the back of her eyes. In black lingerie, over a bowl of dry cereal, a whole quart of juice at hand, Alice called her wasted life to account. And this was Tuesday: a long way from any weekend.

Sure, this rebellion was general in Haledon and sure she was part of the trend. The kids dropped like flies in the teens and twenties in furious explosions of mortality. They shamed the rear guard, those coming up, and not simply with autoerotic deaths either (those hangings and other asphyxiations), nothing so mon-ochromatic. There was exhaust in closed garages, car crashes, drug overdoses, ritual eviscerations, gun-shots, and self-immolation. They had all seen it all, whatever good that did.

Her hangover skidded over the facts. This band thing. The nuclear blast of her nuclear family.

The house seemed empty. She wondered which of her personal effects she had lost last night. Then, in the middle of the dry cereal, it came to her, the text of Dennis' whispered parting. He would introduce her, if that was what she wanted. She would wait until late evening, and then they would go over. "Meet me in the afternoon," he had said, "we'll kill time."

And she did want to meet Lane. Maybe it was morbid but what the fuck.

Mrs. Smail drove in sheets of rain, high winds, low visibility. Earlier, the sun had overcome the precipi-tation with the ardor of cheap religious illustrations, but the squalls had resumed. She was in Redding—a place she had visited when young, when her father, a steel magnate, had traveled there—and it was a deadly place to land, now, its foundries and factories abandoned. She needed food.

Her gas card was good for another year. Who would notice her absence? There was lunch with the woman whose husband had hanged himself. There was Alice. The details of life slowed and blunted change, and already Evelyn felt her hysterical resolve waning. But for now she was in a diner. At scorched Formica counters, woeful travelers with fatigued expressions and unpressed clothing consumed inedible fare. She nursed her boiled coffee and ate her sandwich as those around her did. Turkey on white bread, drenched in a mulatto gravy, fouled with hunks of undissolved flour—the house specialty. No one spoke. As Evelyn ate, though, she eyed the wall phone by the dilapidated rest rooms. Its old rotary dial beckoned. She guessed that the lives of the men and women she had known over the years—in the Garden State and out in the open spaces—were largely given over to sudden departures and humble returns. Marriage and divorce were like that, for example. Everywhere things looked better everywhere else. Everywhere a hunger for some simple old conversation.

In the neighborhood where Dennis and Alice walked the row houses ran in diagonals. The freight rails demarcated the endpoints of these line segments, sheered them off. The houses, in sensational and inexpensive colors—lavender, pink, magenta—abutted the empty factory spaces in Haledon, that part of town where dumps, ominous enclosures, loft spaces, warehouses coexisted with bars and after-hours clubs, places like Dover's, Go-Go's, Bottled Blondes. Beware of Dog signs abounded in the neighborhood, electrical fences, house alarms that cried the word *burglar*. In a delta on the Dern River—that waterway that idled desultorily through town—men with hangdog expressions presided over the city car pound. Short of fingers with which to reckon their crude mathematics, they vivisected the machines, stripped off the erotic curves of fenders, tail fins, hood ornaments, and resold them to those residents of Haledon who seemed to spend the entire spring attacking the undersides of cars with rusty tools. Ancient towtrucks brought a steady stream of raw material.

This was the neighborhood where Alice and Dennis wasted the afternoon. Here, the washers and dryers had lifetimes of hourly wage in them. It was a good neighborhood for plumbing. Dennis was here often. Up on the heights, where the plumbing was newly installed, the fixtures were like burnished hand mirrors. No septic tank explosions, no clogs or floods troubled the affluent.

And he told Alice he had come here a lot when he was younger, during his stint at night school, just for the walk. The rain fell steadily and dully upon them. The streets, and the playground at the end of the block, had emptied. In Haledon the playgrounds were fashioned almost entirely from abandoned car tires. Where the two of them walked, shattered glass speckled the streets—car windows and beer bottles. On another day, sunlight would find innumerable reflectors here. There would be a devotional beauty to the destruction. Not today.

A car with missing headlights accelerated through a four-way stop sign. Dennis and Alice walked left and then right and then left. All the streets were identical. They arrived back at the van through heading away from it.

Dennis opened the passenger door for Alice. He went around back to make sure the tools and instruments of his trade were all in place, and when accounted for, he jumped in front.

"I'm not saying right now or anything," he said, "but you could go a long way in here. In this van."

Alice didn't say anything.

In silence, they drove up the winding lane that traversed the cliffs, a road where abandoned cars were turtled and the pavement was cluttered with flattened roadkill.

After the Mexican food, Dennis took her back to his parent's place, the stately three-storied house about a mile down the street from where Alice lived. They walked around the back of the garage, padding silently around a coil of bright green hose, around emptied trash barrels. More rain fell. A few outdoor lights illumined their passage. By the door to the laundry room, Dennis pointed at the wood pile by the low section of roof line. They were going to climb.

"It can't be done any other way," Dennis said.

"Come on. The garage door is open. What's the big deal?"

"If you want to do it, you have to do like I say. Certain things, certain ways."

He smiled and she just let it go. He boosted her up.

Across the splintering windowsill, they landed with muddy feet on a worn, pale blue carpet in the second floor hallway. When they knocked at the door on the end, a frail voice replied. Alice wiped her hands on her miniskirt.

Poorly lit by a single bedside lamp—a lamp which cast terse shadows across the angles of the dresser, the bookshelf, the wooden stool, the open closet door —amid blankets piled and twisted as if in a washer cycle, Lane stirred slightly, facing away.

"Hey," Dennis said.

Lane didn't say anything.

"What's going on?" Dennis fell onto the stool by the window. "I mean—uh—we were just killing time and we thought we'd drop in."

He rolled over. His hand emerged from under the covers long enough to fuss with them. The hand was ordinary enough, but Alice studied it, and studied his skeletal face, his wasted blue eyes.

"This is Alice from down the street," Dennis said.

"Nice to meet you," said Lane.

A freight train was passing outdoors, wailing. Dennis found a joint in his pocket.

"You're really down," Alice prompted. She settled on the floor by the bed. Over her shoulder the moon hung between clouds. "I've seen this before."

Lane didn't say anything for a while, and then he asked Dennis not to smoke the joint, or at least to open the window.

"Huh?"

"Come on," Lane said.

The sense of the request finally came to Dennis and he rushed to stub the joint out on the sole of his boot. He wasn't thinking, really. There was something horrible about the whole situation.

"I used to imagine," Alice said, "that I was going to quit breathing and suffocate. That's what I thought. I know you can't, but that's what I thought."

Lane fixed a stare upon her. "Anatomical dolls," he said. "That was you, right?"

Alice smiled.

"Listen," he said, "if I was feeling conversational or something. I don't know—"

Lane looked away. He watched the clock on the bedside table, inches from his eyes, the radar sweep of the second hand. Flight of days.

"Hey well we were just on our way out," Dennis said, "we were just leaving. Sorry to bother, really, bro."

Alice, on her knees by the edge of the bed, reached to shake his hand. Through erroneous shadows, amid uncomfortable furnishings, his touch was foreign, stern and lifeless at once.

At the edge of the driveway, where a police cruiser

was passing and every third streetlamp flickered weakly, Dennis and Alice traded summarizations.

"No big deal," Alice said. "There's been lots worse. I bet Mike Maas was worse than that."

They lingered silently over Mike.

"Lane won't take it so bad that we came in," Dennis said, "he won't even remember we were there."

"Yeah, no big deal."

There were puddles in the crumbling pavement. The reflection of the streetlamps played on wet surfaces. Their distorted reflections fluttered in spring breezes.

"Can we go back to your place?" Dennis said.

"You mean—"

It was a stupid question. The failures of a whole year flowered around them.

"Can't I?"

"No way," Alice said. "I'm going over to see Scarlett. Give it a rest for a couple of days, okay?"

"Wait," Dennis said. "Hold on. Lemme just drive you—"

"Forget it," she said. She smiled when she said it.

They stood like that for a second, hands dug deep in empty pockets.

Mrs. Smail, seated on a bed that did not give to her figure, a bed with Magic Fingers, was looking at the black rotary phone she had placed beside her. She was in Bristol, P.A., a town composed entirely of chain franchises. She was going back, though. Tomorrow she would cross back into the Garden State, having forsaken this foolishness, this cut-and-run, this duck-and-cover. With trepidation she would return, like a missionary crossing over deconsecrated ground, in wide arcs. All that mattered right now was how she missed home, with its steady diet of appointments and responsibilities. The busy tireless comfort of routine.

She searched her purse for her address book, a ruined old alligator cover with a broken binding, containing all names and scraps from her life. It was missing. Finally she overturned the purse on her bed, and methodically searched through the piles of neatly folded notes to herself. There was so much of her life in the pile, so much of the thick accumulation of life. Just before she found the address book, crammed into a corner of her billfold, she unfolded a tattered note in pale yellow:

DRUMMER WANTED.
ORIGINAL MATERIAL.
CALL ALICE.
LEAVE MSSGE.

2 / L.G., Nedd, and Antonio started the band with three numbers they were permitted to showcase at a Parent's Day offering at Haledon High. They were slotted between a recitation and a scene from a romantic comedy. They rehearsed evenings in the band room, running through the same chords, one four five, one four five, knocking down sheet music stands with their instruments, scribbling obscenities across the music staff blackboards. Sometimes truants outside, underneath the window, drank beers and clapped sporadically.

L.G. led the three of them through cursory examinations of song structure and rhythmical variation. Verse, verse, chorus, bridge, verse, chorus, chorus. He stretched his voice for the falsetto demands of the period. On the downbeats, he jumped. His fingers blundered across the dotted chords of beginners' manuals.

It didn't matter what they played, really. It was something in the bloodstream. All that mattered was the colored lights that flickered over their exhortations. From red to green on the cymbal crashes, from green to blue on the high fast part of the solo L.G. had labored to reproduce from a record.

And then he decided maybe a girl. Yeah, there was one who hung out on the loading dock some days. This was how it seemed to have happened later. She was a little older. A girl could reach high notes and plus there was the commercial appeal of girls.

When they played the auditorium, they played for eight minutes. Three songs, eight minutes. By the end of the first song the kids were on their feet. It was simple, unadorned rebellion, that ovation. The kids didn't like love odes or musical comedy unless it was four-four time. L.G. sang the first two songs, and then Alice came on to sing one. A job well done.

Next, the prom. Fresh from success. They had so little material they did a medley of songs with the same chords, you know, like E-A-B, over and over. They played for thirty-five minutes, modulating once in a while when they had to, maybe G-D-E: "Devil on the Devil Train," "(Baby Talks) Sign Language," "Out in the World," "Maybe Maybe," "Last One Out of Town," and "West of Network."

Alice wrote a song, and L.G. wrote an instrumental called "Voodoo," and there were a couple of other, pretty mediocre originals, but the prom was a home-town crowd. They ate it up. Alice meant every word. She was a medium, an intercessor.

Soon they were rehearsing in a desolate factory space and calling each other at night with contradictory ideas, fantasies of success. Fly-by-night businesses inhabited the warehouse by day—the doors had fading stencils on them that read Cut-Rate Plastics, E.Z. Dispatchers, Lady's Sports Apparel. Alice got the band name from reading a note on the elevator there.

When Antonio quit showing up, L.G. persuaded Alice to break the news to him, but L.G. did the hiring of Nick himself. Nick was an animal. When he wasn't drumming he was in a state of suspended animation. He spent days at the filling station by the Eastern Spur of the Thruway.

Scarlett blew into town that Autumn after L.G. and Nedd got out of high school. The band had been together a year and a half, maybe. She had left things in a mess in the Empire State—or so she said—had bounced from job to waitress job, losing things, filching money from her registers. She moved to Haledon to regroup—she was part of that diaspora from the Empire State. She picked up the bass guitar then, while cashiering at the Farmboy, an island of health food in town. Scarlett committed larceny there, too, of yogurt-covered carob balls and cookies made with carrot and celery juice. But things were different in Haledon. People turned a blind eye to shrinkage. It was that kind of berg.

And that was where Nick met her, in the Farmboy. He watched while other people paid for tofu, dates, kafir, brewer's yeast, baba ganouche. He came in a lot, and made idle conversation with her. And Scarlett, because she was new in town, because she watched television and drank maybe a little too much, because she was trying to put off going back to Ohio, took Nick home with her one night, to her place above the exterminator's business. They slept together on the couch, beneath a ragged overcoat Scarlett had brought east.

Next morning, she tried to get rid of him as quickly as possible. Just looking at him made her homesick. But Nick noticed the guitar case then, and one thing led to another. And Scarlett got back under the overcoat with him, because Nick had said something about rehearsal. Maybe she wanted to anyway, but it cemented the deal.

Anyway, Nedd was joining the armed forces. L.G. was impressed with the fact that Scarlett had once done slide projections for a band in the midwest that featured a singer who later had a major label deal. Alice liked her artificial hair color, her poise. And besides she seemed like the kind of girl who could do math and return phone calls.

That autumn, when another class of kids from high school was heading off to college, taking hand-me-downs and stacks of warped records, Critical Ma$$ had its first series of weekend gigs at Dover's. They had played all the clubs, and it had taken them these two years to move from Tuesday nights to the weekend. L.G. decided to take another year off. Alice decided to work another year in the Pinnacle Coffee Shop. They played Oakland, Tenafly, Stadt, Ho-ho-kus, the Oranges, Trivium, with Scarlett on bass; it was the last incarnation of Critical Ma$$. Scarlett was still with them a year or so later, when the kids started to drift back from trade school, looking for jobs in maintenance or for the railroad, when Nick decided to go to community college, when the band's bookings became rarer and rarer, when they rehearsed just a couple of times a month.

She still lived on the third story over the exterminator's place, and in the evening his window display flickered, illuminating tidy ranks and files of the various over-the-counter toxins and the tee shirts the exterminator had printed up depicting the cartoon torture of cartoon insects. When he was not busy, as he wasn't this night, the exterminator sat out in front of the shop smoking a cigar and taking in the activity on the street. He kept long hours. It was late on Wednesday when he folded his folding chair at last, stubbed out his cigar and descended the four steps into his storefront. When he emerged again, with a series of deep, rheumy coughs, it was to padlock the gate and to head home.

Scarlett sat in the window above. It was night. This weekend the clocks would jump forward and on Easter Sunday it would be like the sun would never set. Now Scarlett turned from the window, slid the bass guitar back in her lap. The television was set on the coffee table, and beside it a martini glistened as if in a magazine pictorial.

The buzzer sounded. Harsh and unexpected. Scarlett moved the bass and stepped over the television cord dangling between the table and the wall. But then she advised herself to stay put. She snatched up the martini, sipped it, replaced it on the table. She decided to establish the identity of the intruder. She stuck her head, again, out the window. Breezes blew.

It was Alice, of course, and Scarlett unhooked her house keys from a beltloop and flung them out.

As Alice entered, Scarlett passed her eyes furtively over her guest's fashions. Black leather jacket, torn denim miniskirt, black fishnet stockings, black lipstick, white face powder, red plastic earrings. Scarlett felt that she lacked the throw weight to be Alice's friend.

"Want a drink? I'm just having one myself."

Alice nodded and they arranged themselves on the couch. The television picture scrolled around. Drinks came and went and came and went. Scarlett yawned and picked at the bass guitar in her lap. They told the story of the band. So much hyperbole. Alice scapegoated L.G.; she told Scarlett about Dover's the night before. Scarlett called him a thug, but she really said it only for Alice. And then she told her how he had called her, too, about the party, the April Fool's Party. They accused him of crimes like musk and leopard-spotted briefs. They spoke of his covetous love of pit bulls and championship wrestling and leisure suits.

And then Scarlett began on Nick.

"A grease monkey," she said, "lube jobs are about the most complicated things he understands. Could jumpstart a car but that's about all. He sure doesn't know how to jumpstart a girl. The things he—"

And then she just stopped.

"Well, but he played okay," Scarlett said.

They sipped their drinks.

"But that's over."

"Yep," Alice said.

A sitcom took up dead air. It slipped its picture again and the figures spun end over end, aimlessly.

"Do you want to play Saturday? At the thing?"

"Oh, I don't know," Alice said. "What would we play?"

They drank.

Scarlett got up, tripping on the television cord, unplugging it, plugging it back in. She wandered around her apartment, straightening things. From the couch to the sink, to freshen their beverages, from the sink to the closet, where she searched for and found a pair of extra pillows and a light summer blanket, back to the sofa, loaded down with bedding, symbol of kindness and concern, she moved with a domestic fervor. Scarlett believed this was what she did best, and while she labored she slipped into a state of dreamless sleepwalking. It was nice.

"What the fuck are you doing?"

"Aren't you going to stay over? You don't want to go all the way back up the hill at this hour. It'll take forty-five minutes. You can sleep on the couch here."

Alice shook her head violently. "Shit, no. You don't get it, Scarlett. I'm gonna take the bus back."

"Oh, come on."

"Yessir."

Alice handed her the glass. She was out of the sofa as though it were aflame. Within seconds Alice was backing down the stairwell, and Scarlett was waving the half-empty tumbler.

From Scarlett's house to her own after midnight on a Wednesday was probably faster walked, but you'd have to traverse the cliffs, traverse that festering wood, and it was all uphill. So though the buses only came every half hour between ten and two, Alice sat on the bench on the corner waiting. She watched Scarlett's lights go out. She watched the traffic on the streets vanish.

When would the night come when she wasn't out waiting like this, when she didn't worry about passing out on the bus or losing her keys, or puking, or saying something ridiculous? When would she stop forgetting to get into bed or to undress? A lot of stuff that had receded when she first threw a switch on an amplifier just never would come back now. But there were things that were still okay, like when the tiny wizened bus driver opened the doors at last, she asked him if he would wake her when they reached the heights, and he nodded and smiled.

Either direction on the Garden State Parkway gave way only to commerce and industry, uninterrupted by natural scenery, so Mrs. Smail gas-pedaled her European performance automobile up over the speed limit, and ran out along the western edge of the state from Trenton to Suffern, in a gentle but persistent aside.

The road was lined with a profusion of trees and shrubbery, antique stores and roadside vegetable stands, florists and general stores, though it was not far either from the handgun factory and the place where they decaffeinated coffee with nuclear fission. But no one would be timing her on her way to her destination, so Evelyn dawdled before encountering the Thursday afternoon rush.

She was stuck. Something in her mind was not made up. It seemed natural. Hardship and confusion and quiet desperation seemed natural. In just this way the back road on which she slalommed across the Garden State's halfhearted hills, with its langorous turns and vistas, emptied out suddenly onto the Thruway. Stoplights, fast food joints, auto franchises, carbon monoxide, outlet stores, artificial shrubbery and cedar chips, garishly painted trash receptacles. Nothing but commerce from here on out.

All this happened right at the time New Jersey was repealing the law banning self-serve gas stations within its boundaries. Their arrival touched the crusader in Mrs. Smail. She disliked the effort involved, the bulletproof encasements, the shuddering metal drawers and microphones. Nevertheless they were here to stay now, those military bunkers. And when Mrs. Smail veered from the thruway to fill her tank, she encountered the self-serve arrangement again. She was considering some grass roots resistance program as she shut her car off; she would spearhead the movement as soon as she got back to town.

Evelyn crossed the island of gas pumps and arrived at the attendant's booth, waving a five.

"Premium," she said.

The clerk's cold, electrified, accented English crackled through the intercom. He asked her to speak up. He pointed at the microphone area.

"Premium," she said, and emboldened, "and what if I'd like to have the oil changed?"

The clerk shrugged.

She asked if it was a partial service island, if he would change the oil.

He pointed with the magic marker he was using to fill out a word search puzzle. He pointed at the island of pumps. "Rag. Right over there."

Mrs. Smail raised her braceleted hands. She told him she didn't know how. She told him she didn't even know how to start.

The clerk shook his head.

"Just show me how," she said.

She launched the five dollar bill summarily into the sliding metal tray, and headed back to the car, certain that he would follow. And he did, locking the bunker with a mammoth clump of keys.

While the pump was secured in the on position—Mrs. Smail did it herself after opening the hood—she stood off to one side as he cleaned the dipstick contemplatively.

"Looks fine," he said. "Everything fine."

And just then, as he completed his work, Mrs. Smail's car, according to obscure and hieroglyphic circuitry that would never be fully understood, through a menacing convergence of machines and chance, engaged by itself. Though parked, at a dead stop, it engaged and moved swiftly to top speed.

Mrs. Smail was lost in thought, thinking of home, when it happened, palms pressed against the driver's window. She was caught in a moment of mild contentment. She was propelled backwards, whether by centrifuge or by psychic forces. The attendant was propelled backwards, too, tripping over the service island, stumbling. The hood slammed shut as the car bore left—poorly aligned—onto the Garden State Thruway. As it struck a luxury car in the passing lane, Evelyn Smail reached over the prone body of the station attendant. She pressed her ear to his chest.

Next, the car bounced as it encountered the lane divider, bounced, hit another car, and then a third. The car roared like angered wildlife. Mrs. Smail sat on the pavement, beside the unconscious body of the attendant.

When the police arrived soon after, the traffic was already backed up into the middle of the state. Both Mrs. Smail and the attendant were hustled into an ambulance. Traffic helicopters registered the lengthy rubbernecking delays.

The fifth day back brought Lane, if not improvements of outlook, at least mobility. The objects in his bedroom made him sick. They finally drove him out. He had made trips to the bathroom in the last few days, actually nauseous at the prospect of recollection, nauseous at the sight of old photos on his bookshelf, at his old belongings, his furniture. When he could not move from bed, his mother turned up. His stepfather came once and spoke of joists.

He read nothing, watched no television, listened to nothing but the clamor of birds. He waited for a great flattening to come, through his mother's goodwill, from some medication she kept in the bathroom. He had not suspected her of keeping drugs around but now she brought pills and grape juice and he swallowed them down. The drugs hacked off the tops and bottoms of him. He was lopped off, without vertigo and chills and panic, without sensation of any kind. He could walk around.

By the doorway he shivered, fumbling in the chest of drawers until he found an old pair of ill-fitting bell-bottoms. He dragged them on over his ridiculous briefs, slid into an unpressed shirt and some slippers, preparing for his cup of coffee as though securing it were the act of an adventurer.

"Breakfast?" Ruthie said—nervously, delicately—when he turned up, as though he had never left. "Coffee? Cereal? Banana?"

He said nothing.

"Well, it is nice to see you."

Nothing.

"I have imported coffee. It's half something and half something else. Java or mocha something."

"I don't know," Lane said.

"Tea then? How about it? That might be best anyway. Don't want to pour too much into the system. Don't want to overdo it."

She lit the gas under the kettle without reply. She chose a teabag, an herbal brand.

Outside the sun emerged temporarily.

Ruthie thought: down the block there had been a couple whose daughter suffered from some kind of mental illness. They were a quiet, intense pair. They struggled with the daughter for a long time. Struggled because what else was there to do? The husband had admitted one night to sleeping at the foot of the stairs, in a tangle of blankets, hoping to wake if their daughter tried to leave the house. Sleeping sometimes, mostly just lying there in a state of panicky concern. Waking with muscle pains of every hue. In her mania, he hoped, the daughter would not have had the sense to try and step over him. Or he would withstand the trampling and lead her back to bed. Ruthie remembered how they had all discussed it in the neighborhood, at parties, in chance encounters. The toll it took was most costly when you were no longer aware of it. You developed these peculiar muscles. And then the girl had taken her life anyway.

"I'll go later," his mother said. "I'll go out later."

Lane nodded.

He had got thinking about drugs. It was the medication. Just remembering—the bad times especially. Good times on drugs were hard to pin down. On his fifteenth birthday he had sat in a pine bluff on the hill above town and swamped himself with his first sixpack. Energy had exploded from those cans. Sixpacks were the cold fusion of personality. With sixpacks he welcomed himself into the industrial age.

Hashish had tasted like peat moss. Nothing happened at first. This was December. After the first sixpack. He headed into the trees exuberant, just to be in violation of federal regulations. He pushed over a dead birch tree and watched it thunder down the hill, taking down branches and underbrush, narrowly missing a car on the road below. Simple cause and effect. It started to snow. When the hash hit, the snow was just beginning to fall. It was unbelievably complicated that snow. He pondered the intricacies of flakes, down to their infinite miniatures. It confounded him. He lay face down in the snow. He shoveled the stuff into his mouth.

There was a story like this for every drug. It took a

couple of years, but he ran through the better part of the available list. Angel dust, mushrooms, acid, cocaine, reds, quaaludes, speed, and then heroin. Max, his pal, had volunteered to tie him off one time, to hit those tributaries, and he let him do it. Doing dope was like driving on an expressway for the first time. It was like driving fast on the New Jersey Turnpike. But just that one time.

Acid was the best. It was the thing most in his mind for a while, better than imagined sexual encounters, better than books or records, or being the smartest guy in high school. Lane lived to trip. He wanted to trip permanently.

There was a time out in the golf course, loaded on a half dozen hits of something or other, some acid someone had cooked up in a basement. There was that placebo effect. Always a bad sign. Within twenty minutes he was seeing things. Meteor craters eight feet deep in the surfaces of the fairways, craters in the shape of the human eye. In the shape of a stylized eye. Wait, he was down in one of the craters and was crossing it, pacing off its dimensions. He rubbed his hands in the moist soil that was loosened by the impact of the meteor. Spacious as a fresh grave. And right then, there was the sound of other interments around him: last rites, dirges, weeping relations. From above, the first handful of dirt was heaped down upon him. From above, the burial party peered down on him. Fifty feet up. In the vast heavens that spread over them, shooting stars. Shooting stars like the particles colliding in an accelerator. Shooting stars like charmed subatomics.

He was open-field running when he climbed out of there. He was sprinting past animals grazing, backwards through the past—there were mammoths, horses with cloven hooves, the usual hallucinatory stuff, all of it true—and he just kept running. He was on a narrow suspension bridge with frayed lines. Crumbling cliff faces. A little panicked, but hoping it was just edgy. Were those the lights of the golf clubhouse? What had happened? How did he get this way?

Beyond the clubhouse was the road, beyond the road the trees, through the trees a church, within the church a minister who would answer if he knocked. But there was an elongation of moments before that knock. It took hours to reach the rectory and even then he couldn't knock, even if he wanted nothing else. He shivered on the step, waiting. Imponderable ideas swarmed around him, and they had actual shapes and velocities like moths on the outside of a screen door. He shivered on the step until the church door swung back of its own and all that was left was to announce himself. He launched himself into the arms of the minister, raving.

Five, six, seven hours he lay underneath the small breakfast table in the rectory kitchen. That was when Lane learned that time was a rigor learned only in the outermost layer of civilizing thought. He remembered only a few images—a giant tangled rose bush whose bloom was shaped into a human mouth from which spasmodic groans of erotic release issued forth. That kind of thing. God actually appeared to Lane that night—or maybe it was just the holy spirit—to tell him his torment was justified.

And then when the voices had cleared from his head—right on schedule because after all that it was just the drugs—the minister had given him a ride back to the house. And then he stood on the front step there, too, frozen, scorched by some literal, caustic acid.

Ruthie asked him if he wanted sugar or milk or lemon or what.

"Whatever."

She wrung the teabag out over the mug.

"Have you seen your brother?"

"No," Lane said.

The kettle rattled on the stove. Steam rose from his mug. He blew on it according to habit.

"He and that girl from down the street were up last night," Lane said. "They came up to my room."

Ruthie spooned her own tea, slowly, absently.

"He sees her," she said. "That's Alice."

The tea scalded him. He didn't really do anything about it. "They came in off the roof."

"Oh. The roof. What was that about?"

Lane didn't say anything. He didn't meet her eyes.

"Now isn't that odd," Ruthie set her tea on the table. A plate, a knife, a green pear. The chair clattered backwards. "Because her mother called last night."

He looked away.

"She wants Alice to move out. She's set a date."

Lane nodded.

"Seems they stay home older and older—" but she saw how it troubled him—"Oh, I don't know why . . . Oh, Dear—"

He covered his face with his hands.

Alice stood at the end of the driveway. Breezes, brightness. Proliferation of spring vegetation. Japanese maple. Sumac. Forsythia. Dandelions. Jack-in-the-Pulpit. Clouds scattering into the east.

The mailbox was empty. Its hinges rusted. She had another hangover. She had drunk at home. She had drunk on the way to Scarlett's, at Scarlett's and she had had a shot on the way to bed. Too late in the day, now, to sleep it off.

The phone rang. It would take her nine tollings, just about, if she ran, but she could not run. It was beyond her, in this condition. She took the supermarket circular with her and read it while she walked. There were some bills. One was marked URGENT RETURN REQUESTED. Past the wall phone in the kitchen to the princess model by the lone recliner in the living room. She could put her feet up.

The greeting on the other end was flat and impersonal. Her first thought: talk show host. But then she understood. There was a certain tone to it.

She was asked her name and she admitted it; she was asked if her mother was in fact her mother. She asked when she last saw her mother and she could not remember. By then Alice knew—you usually do —and was interrupting to ask questions of her own. The voice told her that her mother was hospitalized, that her condition was stable—that she was in shock but it was not expected to be serious—and that her car had been lost on the Garden State Thruway.

The home phone number was ascertained from the contents of the handbag found among Mrs. Smail's valuables at the site of the accident.

Alice nodded.

"Would you like to take down the room number?"

"Sure," Alice said, "lemme just get a pencil. Just hang on." And she headed for the kitchen. She was running. She ran around the kitchen. No pencil. She ran upstairs. There wasn't a pencil in the house. There wasn't a laundry marker. But she found a crayon finally. It was melted into her sculpture. Raw umber. She scraped the waxy fragments from the metal struts of the sculpture and headed for her mother's bedroom, for the telephone there.

Lane overheard his mother on the receiver. The news became clear to him even in fragments; it was like shrapnel working its way to the surface of a wound. He figured the news was dire, but he felt nothing about it.

"Oh, no," Ruthie was saying.

She spoke softly, soothingly. Lane remembered these vowels and assonances and how they had put all worry out of his mind in childhood, and later when his father had become ill. It worked for a while and then it stopped working. A period followed when his mother's kindness disgusted him. Now he saw right through her assurances, but he needed her anyway. Another sad thing about getting older.

"Oh, Alice," Ruthie said.

Alice's parents were divorced, like his, but he recognized the coincidence and set it aside. He thought maybe sometime he would try to say something, but not yet. He was too tired now.

Ruthie set the phone down, and picked up the pen and pad on the counter. Lane was organizing his blanket around his shoulders, getting ready, in this garb, to climb the stairs and get back in bed. Without news of the particulars. He stood. He slid his chair back under the table.

"I guess I'll have to go to see her. She wrecked that car of hers."

Lane nodded. His mother's face was pale and troubled.

He started up the stairs.

*　　*　　*

Dennis abandoned Haledon at lunchtime on Wednesday, careening down the hills toward the edge of Paterson, out near Boonton, out where the Dern River flung itself off from the mighty Passaic, out by that rocky strait of whitewater and falls. A hydroelectric generator there fueled Paterson, all of its industries—the Colt pistol factory, the Krakatoa coffee factory. There was a seafood joint by the river called DD's. Every good no-account lunched there.

Dennis went every couple of weeks. Lots of guys from the county showed now and then. Plumbers, railroad linemen, truckers, phone people—DD's was known statewide for its drinks and congenial lowdown atmosphere. One time it used to be Daniella's or Dmitri's or some foreign name, but now only the preliminary letter remained on the neon sign, though in word of mouth the consonant had doubled, piled up, mated, squared, like an initial stammer. Now it was DD's.

Beside the food and drink, which wasn't much, they sold controlled substances. It was part of the charm. The usual nasal or intravenous stuff, the occasional shipment of something really wild. Everything was padlocked in an old rusted beer cooler at one end of the bar. No one drank beer at DD's anyway. They drank the hard stuff. They smoked a lot. It was an old-fashioned place. The opacity of the air dimmed the already gloomy lighting. You could barely read the selections on the jukebox in DD's. You could barely see your friends.

Dennis was thinking about Alice as he pulled in. He was thinking how he was going to paint her. She sprawled in his mind in portraiture. She was like a vine on the trestle in his mind, like water splashing along a gutter. She wouldn't sit still. A knot of desire cramped in his abdomen, and after it a pall of inadequacy. She would never let him paint her. Even if she did, so what? He closed the door of the van behind him as though it were brittle, in danger of breakage.

All this rain and there would be more, and so Mike and Annie, the owners of DD's, they kept the deck in back closed. In fact the deck was rarely open, as though the view of the falls, the view of its natural energy—its relentless activity—would disturb that deep freeze in DD's. Through small filmy windows, Dennis could just make out the smoldering hydroelectric plant, the smokestacks volcanic, effulgent. It was best to keep the mind of industry at lunch, anyway. Dennis slid onto a stool at the bar.

The raucous noise of the same old jukebox selections, the chiming of empty glasses: Dennis felt at home. This rumbling, this disaffection, this destruction. Chin propped in palm, he waited for Mike to minister to him, and soon enough he lumbered down along the bar. Mike wore blue-black hair down around his shoulders and muttonchop sideburns. Black jeans, fishnet tee shirt, paunch, gold tooth. He set the usual in front of Dennis without acknowledgement.

And then someone called. His own initial D rang out like more of the same. He peered into the murk. In back, where the booths were lined up, he saw Max waving furiously. Max from Haledon. Max the cable television repairman. Max the dealer. He waved Dennis over and moved his tool belt from beside him. Max introduced him to the husky girl sitting across from himself. Jones, his assistant.

"Never seen you here before," Dennis slid in.

Max said, "you kidding me? This place is like the

shelter from the storm. There's cable guys from three states coming in here."

Annie slipped plasticized menus on the table without a word, and Max snapped them up and handed them out.

"What's good?" Jones muttered.

"Burger, Jones," Max said. He was sweating too much. He grinned wildly wherever there was an opportunity. Dennis couldn't figure it out. "That's what there is here. Burgers."

Max Crick was Lane's buddy from Haledon High. They had parted back then; they grew up far apart, did all the pertinent maturation far apart, as people seemed to do. But at one time, they had ruled the clubs—Alice had told Dennis all this—the Electronics Club, the Scifi Club, the Chemistry Club. They had ruled a crowd of losers, the acne-scarred, the drug addicts and teetotalers, kids who had been abandoned or smothered or neglected or disciplined. The guy with one leg shorter than the other, the idiot-savant who was a crossword puzzle prodigy. Dennis remembered them from around the house, from when Lane brought them home. Everybody who was nobody was Lane's friend.

That was the other Haledon High. Same entrances and exits, but nothing like the one Dennis attended. Lane and Max had these people around them and it worked for a while. But somewhere along the line Max absented himself. He started fixing things. He read circuit diagrams, troubleshooting manuals. He explored all topographies marked NO USER SERVICEABLE PARTS. He was good with cars, with carpentry, with cauterizations. Something happened, though, or maybe a lot of small things happened. And no one much hung out with him after that. Except for this Pennebaker. This black guy. All they knew was Max drove this convertible around town by himself. He blasted really hardcore stuff on his car stereo. He drugged himself. He ran the car into a telephone pole and shattered his jaw. Had it wired back together. Saved for two years working as a neon technician. Bought another car. Lost the job. Drugged himself. Lost another car. Lost his license. Got it back. Became a cable television guy.

Dennis had heard all this. Lane told Dennis about Max calling him up after a year of silence. This was after Lane went off to college. And the two of them going for a walk up in the woods. Max was shooting this speed, and Lane was snorting it, and they walked all the way out and back, because neither of them could drive. Walking in the woods, and Max had some-thing to say, but he wasn't saying it. It was always like this.

The burgers came in straw baskets lined in foil. There were no dishes, nothing that needed to be washed. The beers came just after. The jukebox played West of Network again, and then a new song everyone liked. It was a metal ballad. It was this new thing, Sensitive Metal.

Max was itching to say something. He was squirm-ing. He had something in his veins. Squirming and smirking. But Dennis kept his mouth shut. No con-versation got off the ground. It was another one of those days. Then Max brought up Lane. The inevit-ability of it bugged Dennis.

"Maybe gotta get together with the old guy. Gotta, I guess."

It was noncommital. Dennis nodded. He was struggling with his hamburger. Jones struggled, too. They kept falling apart, the burgers. No condiment would bind them.

"This guy's bro, Jones," Max said. "Best of buddies, him and me. Go way back. Way back."

Max waved his hands around. Dennis swallowed, took another bite. "Stepbrother," he said, mouth full.

Conversation lapsed.

Around two, most cleared out of DD's. Max and Dennis and Jones stayed behind, hunkered down, like cardplayers. The commotion of payment and departure distracted the crowd, and amid this distraction, Max set a small plastic zip-loc bag on his Garden State map placemat. A dozen tiny pink pills, the whole batch no larger than a pencil eraser. They had the imperfect shapes of homemade manufacture: they weren't rounded or stamped with milligram strength.

At one time Dennis would not have asked about the contents of the bag, would have simply swallowed what was proffered. At one time he ingested things on no more than the rumor of disorientation—nutmeg, morning glory seeds; in this period he guzzled vanilla extract, feigned stomach ailments in hopes of having paregoric administered. And the allure of the flimsy zip-loc bag and its contents was strong. He hadn't done Dust in maybe three years, but still. It was the times, it was the weather, it was the way things seemed to be going lately.

"I thought this was like for unemployed guys and lobotomy cases and stuff."

Max named a price. Cheap, cheap, he really needed clients.

"No way," Dennis said. "Three for the price of two. Otherwise, no way."

"Jones, you in on this?"

She nodded.

"Peanuts," Max said, he leaned over the table like a true professional. "Look, she's willing to go the distance. Couple of bills. Big deal."

Dennis felt a clump of singles in his pocket, and he set them on the table. "What the fuck?" he said.

"A-O-K," Max said, counting out the tiny pills on the table, splitting the whole pile into three discreet portions. "A-fucking-okay." They stood.

Dennis was driving when it overwhelmed him. He was trying to drive back to a condo conversion where he was putting in the new showers and fixtures. He had thought he would simply do the fixtures the way he was, but when it hit him he pulled over into an empty lot in Paterson.

The radio was playing in the van. He threw open the doors and his eyes passed lazily over cracks in the asphalt, words painted there. Couldn't read them. Not far away, a fat kid was listlessly shooting baskets at a netless hoop. Dennis' windshield was cellophane. The basketball bounced oddly. Incongruities struck Dennis like actual physical blows in the solar plexus, in the testicles, incongruities of the inanimate. Nothing matched up somehow and he couldn't get comfortable.

The humid air was as sharp as teeth, as constrictive as a vacuum. The unhappy world was raw as exposed nerves. The train sounding in the distance reminded him of turned milk. It was raining. The basketball hit the backboard, bounced from the rim, and escaped from the fat kid, who trudged lethargically after it. Dennis noticed all of a sudden, the moiling racket in his guts. When he had been young, he had watched his dog die from swallowing glass; he had watched it howl and run in circles bleeding from mouth and anus, and it was like this all over again, as he made room for unstoppable vomit.

He tumbled out onto the blacktop his palms riddled with splinters as he landed, heaving, spilling. A thick soup spread around him. It burned. It was like puking sterno. He coughed. He wiped his hand on his trousers, on a patch of weeds by his head. He passed out.

Later, the radio chattered. The kid was staring. Dennis tried to shout something but couldn't come up with anything. Again, his stomach. When he was done, he lay stretched on his side. Mister, he heard behind him, yo mister, you okay? The footfalls passed away. Soon he was dragging himself up against the front tire and surveying the parking lot. How long had it taken? A ballad was playing on the radio and it nurtured him. The melody of the song seemed to swing from verse to chorus like the sweet movement of a cradle. Then, he went under again. But, slowly, the afternoon light cheered him. The clouds were dramatic. He was well enough to drive.

As he sat behind the wheel, readying himself, he tested his powers of concentration. With everything he could muster, he listened to the traffic report. Snarl on the Garden State Thruway. Driverless car, driverless car, police clearing the scene.

Ruthie drew back the lion's head knocker. The paint was peeling badly at the Smail's house. Some people's lives drew near to tragedy. In fact, they clotted the suburbs. They spoke at parties, these ones, only of nuclear stockpiles, beaches littered with severed hands, industrial spills, space junk, designer drugs, and all who had died in extremis. Ruthie wanted to shake them by the shoulders and remind them of the moment after their marital vows, of their graduations, of their first infatuations or of bird calls and uncontrollable laughter, but she knew too how sympathetic she was to their point of view. Lower down, Ruthie loved disaster.

She knocked on the door again.

Lane had blinders on now. He had eliminated all but a tiny extract of memories. If she sat him down and reminded him of his smile as a young boy, or when he stood for the first time, or when he spoke his first words, he would deny all of it. He would call attention to all horrible things—his father's disease, every blunted incoherent syllable his father had uttered since his institutionalization, and he himself would duplicate these monosyllables with the rich oratorical precision of the abandoned.

She started around the side of the house, looking for another way in.

She had visited her exhusband—this was after they had parted in law, five or six years after—and upon entering the room where he lay (oblivious as some single-cell thing), she felt at first a twinge of contentment. She wasn't proud of it, but couldn't deny it either: for a moment the end of his long slow decline seemed just fine. But the destitution of his illness worked its way mainly into small delicate histories, and it was in sitting there, watching him breathe that she realized these stories were gone. The story of her marriage was gone, one side of it. She forgave him most things. The loss of a father ruined a boy. And after that day, it seemed to her that all the fathers in the neighborhood were gone. Well, there were fathers, but there were no *dads*.

With Evelyn Smail's wreck, the result would be the

same. Alice would come due. Lane was a good example. He had tried to hold it together in those teen-aged years when a father is so valuable—the obstruction and censure of a father—but Ruthie had seen the seams. His was a life established through guesswork.

By then the progenitor was strapped down nights to keep him from wandering. He became disoriented in the corridors, barging into the rooms of the others. He begged for help with the wordlessness of infancy, bobbing aimlessly in the doorways muttering about wanting to go home, wanna go home, until he stopped even that, until it was a simple wordless want.

So Ruthie had gone for a visit herself. And before she left, she was holding her exhusband's head. It was about as heavy as a lap cat; it was about as heavy as a briefcase. She couldn't stop herself from holding him. Who could have? Proof enough that we marry unto death. She told him he was already home, that everything would be all right.

The garage door at the Smail's house opened like a crypt. Stillness prevailed. Ruthie marveled at the array of gardening tools. She knew for a fact that the Smails had no garden. She tried the door there, the back door. And it was unlocked, and in the living room, Alice lay on the couch, smoking, blowing smoke rings above herself.

Alice said nothing.

Ruthie took Alice's hand and led her to the car, to the passenger side. She went back to check the lock on the garage door.

"Shock," as she climbed into the car again, "there's nothing to it. Things come back in the order they left."

Ruthie's Nova passed around the bank of willows

that swept out onto the edge of the street—those trees had sat there forever; they were like an old ruined paintbrush—along the park and along the cliffs, leaving behind the golf course and the faith-healing church, left onto the avenue that headed out of Haledon. Ruthie drove with a haste appropriate to her mission.

Back in the neighborhood, a police cruiser crawled noiselessly past the Smail residence and vanished. Then Dennis, in his van, took the curve by the willows and drifted into the center of the road, before skidding to a stop at the Smail's driveway, backing up, stalling to a halt. Birds lit on branches and were disturbed by the screech of tires. They lit, again, on electrical lines. Dennis climbed out of the car, as if stumbling from a head-on collision.

Exhausted, he leaned heavily against the garage. Every step brought some kind of aftershock from the drug. Dead reckoning had brought him here. He walked around the perimeter of the house, through the overgrown lawn, expecting to find Mrs. Smail on the porch drinking, expecting to find things as they had always been. But there was no one there. No one answered at the front door. The garage was locked. He pressed his palms against the sheets of glass on the porch. He squinted. He called. Forcing a screen window on the back side of the house, he hoisted himself up and into the dining room. He landed in a heap on the barren, dusty floor.

He traveled around the house as though it were his own. The emptiness of the place satisfied him. He felt better. He had squatter's rights. He was the greatest of explorers. He had survived.

* * *

All over Haledon, as over the nation, Lane observed this movement of need. Addictions, blossoming in personalities like parasites. All over Haledon, kids were coming apart. They bounced back for a while and then they stopped bouncing back, and surrendered to the whisper of their cells. Addiction was the counterintelligence of the flesh, the double-agency. The statistics revealed a swelling outwards, like some kind of ink spill—the guys he knew, and the guys after, just kids, still wet behind the ears, resorting to bad ideas —sexual asphyxia, self-immolation.

And he knew what had happened. It was biochemical transformation. It was genetic engineering. His own body had changed. His body included these substances now the way it had a pancreas or a uvula. There were no turns, tributaries, no parallel lines, no exit ramps, nothing but where this road emptied out. In bed, wasted. His solemn vow, his solemn effort, was to try not to drink while he was on his mother's tranquilizers.

"Just let me sit down for a while," Dennis said coming in now, "just let me talk. I gotta get something off my chest. I just gotta talk."

Lane struggled up from under the quilt. Outside, the sun was slung lower in the trees. Wednesday was gone like the other days.

"You look bad." Lane said. "Are you—"

"Oh, I dunno," Dennis said.

Lane didn't say anything.

"I'm sick as hell." He curled up in one corner, under the window. "Max was over at lunch—"

"Where?"

"Well it was like he had these, you know—"

Lane shook his head.

"Dust. It's Dust," Dennis mumbled.

Lane said, "I didn't even know they still had that stuff."

"I was out in some parking lot. I feel like—"

"How long?"

"Hours, maybe. You did it, right? I thought it was like speed or something. I thought you'd know."

Then they said nothing. Dennis wheezed. It could go on like this a long time.

Lane lifted his quilt up with him as he stood. He walked across the room with it, a risen invalid. He knelt beside his stepbrother and spread the quilt over him. Dennis shook his head and kicked most of it off.

"Max is gonna die," Lane said. "Everybody in this town will. I wouldn't be surprised."

"Yeah and that's not all either." Dennis said, "Just let me have your pillow okay?" Lane plumped a pillow from his bed and then set it under Dennis' head. "Nothing's working out with Alice, that's the thing. Nothing is working out."

Lane didn't say anything.

"I don't know—"

"Well," Lane said, "she'll be pretty wiped out about now. Her mom—"

"What about her mom?"

And Lane told him. And it didn't make much difference, Dennis was going to fall asleep whatever happened, if there was an atomic strike on the Garden State he would have slept. Like his father, Dennis was a born sleeper. And when he did, when he fell unconscious, Lane decided to have another cup of coffee. He felt stronger.

At the nurse's desk, Ruthie Francis recited the information, her arm around Alice the whole time, and

Alice took in the sleek surfaces, high wattages, uniforms, the sound of heels in the corridors.

"You're pale, sweetheart," Ruthie said.

"Face powder," Alice said. "It's always . . . Will she be like in a coma or something?"

Gurneys emerged from the elevator. Bodies. Waxen faces and limbs.

"It's hard," Ruthie said. "I know it's—"

Alice didn't say anything.

"Lane's father has been in the hospital for a long time. My ex-husband."

With visitor's passes displayed, they searched for the room, ventured down dead-ends. No one attended to their comings or goings, though they might have been on a mercy mission or crime spree. The only honest hospital was a locking one, Alice thought.

A hispanic woman occupied the near bed, when they found semi-private room 101A, her face criss-crossed with stitches, her jaw wired shut. A gauzy scrim hung limply between her bed and Mrs. Smail's and above the two of them, on a shared portion of the wall, a pair of television monitors, like technological hanging plants. The hispanic woman was watching a talk show. Alice's mother's television was blank.

Her mother was asleep.

Alice and Ruthie just watched. There were no abrasions or scrapes or sutures upon her. Nothing in her sleep to merit concern. Only the hospital itself was worrisome. It was the place itself that consigned a person to sickness.

Alice understood that the sleep was artificial. Hers was too, pretty often. She understood that she was watching her mother in a drugged state, as her mother had watched her, trying to rouse her for appointments or simply to face things. And she thought she would give it a try again. She would try to improve. Maybe after Easter. She would try to get up early; she would try to get a job.

She sat on the edge of the bed. She shook her mother's shoulder.

"It's me, Mom. Alice here."

Nothing.

"Sure you want—" Ruthie said.

"I don't know," Alice said. She kept shaking her mother's shoulder, but it made no difference. She moved back to a chair by the bed. Alice and Ruthie watched. For a long time they watched. Nurses came and went. The hispanic woman made a phone call. Talk shows on the monitor, and then national news, and then tabloid news.

Scarlett lay in bed now, at the end of the day, having passed the evening again with the television scrolling inscrutably, with drinks, with her bass guitar in her lap. She had fought off the urge to call home, and so the phone lay silently off to one side, unused, with its aide-de-camp, her new answering machine, also unused.

She had put in a few hours at the gourmet shop and it had been humiliating. She had discussed the uses of various herbal medicines with a young engineer who had asked for her number, which she hadn't given him, and then, perhaps in revenge, she had gone out by herself for pizza. And that was it. There was the engineer, and no one else. No wait, she had argued with someone about change. A woman had handed her an odd assortment of change, in order to avoid pennies, and they had argued.

The exterminator had sat in his chair that evening.

She watched him watching the street. The redolence of Chinese food drifted over Haledon, enveloping its thoroughfares. There had been the sound of trains. It occurred to her that if she stayed in Jersey that she would soon be in the employ of the exterminator, wearing his customized tee shirts, recommending this particular toxin.

She decided to take a sleeping pill. Before she had even finished making the decision she was in the bathroom, over the medicine cabinet. Maybe she liked the sleeping pills a little too much. She noticed how the paint was peeling in the bathroom, along the ceiling, as she swallowed. Back in her bedroom, a house fly made impossible right angles unable to find the inch of open window to freedom. Scarlett set the jar of sleeping pills on the floor beside her bed. Angels smiled on the well-rested. God loves sleepers and those who wake.

3 / Max Crick was perishing for what he loved. The seduction of fecal muck in the Garden State's redolent swamplands, the seduction of lovingly pronounced abbreviations of chemical contaminants, the seduction of the fabulous desolation of the Jersey City landfills—blocks of mashed appliances piled like the stepping stones of the great pyramids, swirling tornadoes of airborne scavengers—this seduction had replaced his regular instincts and he was perishing. And he didn't know it.

Plus, spring demoralized him. Daylight Savings Time, morning glories, dogwoods, spangled fritillaries: they moved him like paper cuts or dental abscesses. This was no mating season. Instead, he invited a deep cold to settle in his chest each year at this time and threw himself into the pursuit of his calling—the calling of drug dealer. An interdiction against all reminders of spring. Love in lovelessness only. Anyway, what did he know about alternatives? His mother was six feet under; his brother was locked in a psychiatric hospital outside Bernardsville. There was just the old man, vindictive and lonely. Things might have been otherwise but were not. Max lived in a trailer up in the hills. And he did cable installations. At one time, he trafficked. Not so much now.

The good life wasn't good enough and that was it. The electrician's life. The satellite dish it bought, the stuff in the fridge, the dying house plants. Max lived alone. He had a chemistry set.

He used to hustle rich kids at Go-Go's or Dover's or Bottled Blondes, at the pizzerias and pool halls. When Haledon's rich were unavailable, there were poor kids. Both wanted to score. There was a checklist with which he'd monitored their potential. Have drinks with breakfast? Pillage medicine cabinets at parties? Relax with a copy of the Physician's Desk Reference? Max was available with pats-on-the-back for barside vomiters and rides home for those who drove under the influence, and he had done his job with the nervous excitement of the lover in search of quarry.

His own problems inhibited his successes, though, whittled his profits down to nothing. And now, as he crisscrossed the state, his heart sputtered without igniting; no knife fight or industrial fire or overdose would break through to him. Still, he was not above making a house call now and then. This time to the Krakatoa coffee factory in Paterson.

Flush against the Passaic River, a stone's throw from major highways, with the impermeability of a medieval fortress, the Krakatoa factory had held some allure for Max since boyhood. The desire to break in had moved him powerfully at times, and now, just as he was going to leave powerful desires behind, there was an opportunity. He knew the nightwatchman. The nightwatchman who was now laid off, on his way out and unhindered by obstacles.

At five in the evening the area used to swarm with guys getting off, heading up into the hills to the cheap housing in Haledon, or down into the rundown suburbs, Dint, Fleece, Malagree, Nutley. The factory had manufactured instant decaffeinated coffee, and a smell of scorched rubber or creosoted rooves accompanied its chemical transformations. The smell had sunk into the earth and trees of the area, into the pores of its inhabitants. The Mom and Pop groceries in Haledon and around Paterson carried Krakatoa at the expense of other brands. It was the brand that was not soluble in water, which congealed at the bottom of the cup, but which jumpstarted the nerves, even without the caffeine. Max drank it, like everyone else.

Then they automated the plant. The news was splashed across county papers, but who read those? At that time labor confrontations were routine, and managers fired unions the way others got tattoos or drank in the morning. The controversy was marginal. Soon Krakatoa was indicted for dumping in the Passaic. Nerve-damaging carcinogens, birth-defectors and worse. The factory used a corrosive irradiation process for the removal of caffeine. The grandiosity of it was what Max loved.

Now the factory was a dynastic ruin. Authorities erected a complex barbed wire around it, padlocked most of it, rented the rest to small businesses. Responsible parties vanished. The last working force fell out of sight, inscribed on statistical rolls in the nation's capital. By a third party, not connected with the illegal dumping, or its sanitization, Nails Pennebaker was hired to patrol the place on the swing shift. Nails from

Haledon High, now of Paterson. Max's old friend Nails. Nails the token black. Nails with the nightstick and gun.

They had been blood brothers. They had officialized it, shooting speed in the men's room at Haledon High before speed had caught on in Haledon. It was senior year when no one else would have anything to do with Max. The two of them slept through remedial geometry in the back of the room, pills under their tongues. They had waited for fire dills to ravage official offices, pulling alarms when fed up with waiting. They brought weapons to school, extorted lunch money, tormented special education students, sold misidentified drugs to the unsuspecting and naïve. The would-be's.

But they fought. Nails wasn't comfortable in Haledon. He was behind the lines. Max would say he would meet him in a certain place and then not show up, or show up hours late. And Nails would languish among the whites while Max was halfway across the state, sitting on the cliffs overlooking the bridge or idling in the industrial everglades.

They fought because Max didn't make payments on the shoebox of substances that Nails got for him. He bartered with the underworld collection specialists of Paterson when they appeared, begging to repair things for them, begging to do small crimes. The results were not good. The syndicates vandalized Max's Dad's place, when Max still lived there.

The spring after school Nails gave up and moved into a place of his own in Paterson. His mom and dad had moved into the white suburbs to spearhead a business and they stayed. They didn't want to give up too easily. But infiltration was adulteration the way Nails saw it, and he went back to his hometown to work for

the big guns, the big dealers. He thrust bound packages through mail slots.

He was all politeness to the guys with the nick-
names, but it wore him down after a while, just as
much as if he was pushing a broom for some white
guy. After a while, he became a nightwatchman. It
was a sort of a moral decision, the way Max saw it,
Nails deciding to keep to himself.

Max locked his scooter on the chainlink fence over
by the decoplex movie palace where they showed
slasher films and triple X features. The interstate ran
past. He hiked across the freight tracks, past the bullet-
shaped chemical cars, past the garage operations
which sold tax-free cigarettes and beer. Cars raced
past in every direction. The breeze was chilly and he
liked the walk.

Part of this problem with spring had to do with the
fact that it was this time last year when his brother
committed himself. Not that he cared about his brother
all that much, but it turned out Max missed him. Now
he spoke with his brother on the phone. His brother
laughed about who had come in and how bad off they
were, about who was fucking who; he kept Max up
on drug therapies, and other trends. Shocking was
back in again. But like all the rest of them inside, his
brother was afraid to come out. He would come out
when the insurance money ran out altogether, but not
a day sooner.

The bolts in the factory gate twisted angrily. The
barbed wire wobbled. The smell of industry past, of
wasted potency, permeated the vacant lot in front of
the factory. Nails baton-twirled his nightstick as Max

slipped in. No friendly greetings—Max was just swallowed in.

"Good stuff I got," he blurted out, "big schemes."

And then into the corridor—the fire door swung back with a finality. Inside all was worn and silent.

"Some rockaroll bands rehearsing in here, usually," Nails said, "but not so much anymore. Used to hear 'em at night."

Max knew who. He listened to his sneakers, to Nails' unshined uniform shoes. The only sound.

On the elevator, that metal cage, floor numbers appeared, inched past like flotsam on a sluggish waterway. Nails smoked. Nails told him about his money problems. It wasn't like him. But he told Max everything. He was talking about his kid again. Max had heard from someone else. The kid didn't have thumbs. His wife had taken something during her pregnancy. There was this new drug they had on the market. The thumbs sort of jutted out like little antlers. The saddest thing, the kid trying to pick things up. They were putting him in a special school, when the time came. And that wasn't all. Nails was losing the job at the factory. The story went on and on. It was a slow elevator.

"They're closing up around here."

"But listen," Max said, "I'm onto something here."

"Salesman," Nails said. And then he smoked.

When the elevator stopped, finally, they were on the roof. Evening faded. It was pretty obvious to Max that whatever had bound them together, that furious affection of high school, was gone now. If it was the drugs that caused it, the drugs weren't causing it now. The drugs were all worn out. Nails was preoccupied with all this stuff that Max hadn't even gotten to. And that fact that he was white and Nails was black, it seemed totally different from how it used to be.

Max knew he had his own problems—he couldn't, for example, tell abject terror from erotic obsession (phrases like murder-suicide stirred him in the loins), but to him these problems seemed like good ideas. And the casket of decaffeination was the best he had come up with yet. What was the half life of cesium, anyway? With a blowtorch he would get at the stuff. He just wanted to look at it.

"Talk, Nails," Max said.

Colors swept across the clotted traffic in dappled waves. A slow pulsing of horns sounded on the nearest bridge.

"It isn't the same, Nails," Max said, "that's all."

Nails produced a flask from his back pocket—for a moment it looked like he was reaching for his firearm—and it was the smart kick of bourbon that Max tasted when it came around to him. It should have felt like something was passing between two friends, but it just felt like something was passing away. Max wondered how many inches were in the flask, how much he could drain without being an asshole.

In conversation, he tried to resurrect some of the lost. To make conversation, he talked about Mike Maas and how Mike drove out to the swamps. Max thought about guys in films stumbling around on fire, flaming scarecrows. A lot of conversation in Haledon eventually got back around to Mike Maas.

And then there was Lane:

"Back in town looks like he's dying or something. Like a corpse. Walks around like a ghost. And Alice from Critical Ma$$. Her mother run over a guy and crashed up her car and lost some fingers. The car started by itself."

"By itself." Nails said. "They used to rehearse out here, Alice and them."

They were by the stairwell entrance. Two traffic helicopters crisscrossed through the urgent twilight.

"Listen," Max said. "I really gotta know Nails are we gonna break this thing open or not. I have ideas" —he was searching through his pockets for the bag with the speed in it—"what I mean is I want to know about your gun. What kind of gun they give you on a job like this anyway?"

He shoved pills into Nails' hands.

There was another pint hidden in the emergency closet where the extinguishers used to be. What floor were they on? Nails opened a massive hydraulic door with a series of numerical combinations. In the massive assembly line space, as grand as the public spaces of an ancient empire, Max felt he was on to something. It was probably just the drugs.

"Made planes here in WWII," Nails said. He leaned against a metal cabinet in the doorway and gestured outward across vast expanses.

The room was measureless. Biological. The rusted conveyor rose up into an open mezzanine like entrails stretching from one digestive sluice to another. With the sleek simplicity of tendons and bones, lengths of specialized machines lined the conveyor. They shrunk plastic wrapping around the coffee jars, Max learned, aligned the jars and lidded them. And then there was an ominous looking machine, a sort of steel giraffe, which did nothing more than grind up faulty product, heat it into a molten soup and pour the result into the Passaic River.

But Max was after the biggest machine, the twentieth century machine, and it was in the back under a ledge, as if it were the center of an altar painting. Shrine. Adytum.

"So you gonna give me your pistol or what?" Max said.

"What's my cut?"

"Half of everything, man. Half of my firstborn kid."

Nails sucked on the pint bottle in consideration. Then he exchanged it for the pistol, holstered the stoppered bottle, neck down, handed the weapon over, barrel first.

"That thing's been turned off for years. Pistol ain't gonna do any good at all."

"What's it to you?" Max said quickly, and fired.

Nails crouched under the conveyor as the first three or four shots ricocheted from the surface of the nuclear decaffeinator and glanced from the walls. Max balanced the barrel of the pistol on his forearm, according to the model of television cop shows.

"Let's take a look." He headed for the target, a true rifleman. They fingered the dents in the metal housing of the machine.

"You want to try?" Max asked. Nails simply offered him more ammunition. The next shots inflicted no more damage than the first.

They crowbarred it open later—it wasn't that hard at all—and by that time Max had soaked through his denim shirt. An ancient dust from the factory had seeped into his flesh. They were drunk and wired when the side panel came off, but Max felt the keen wound of the machine's emptiness anyway. No little blue cakes, no perfect poison of dissolution, or clarity. Nothing to be smoked, parceled or snorted.

Was Nails capable of consolation? Max had long since lost the ability to understand their conversation.

Max was joyous and distraught both. Which was which? The modern world was strange and unfinished, an abandoned project. Its effects were subliminal. Max was the kind of guy who would find a neutron bomb explosion beautiful, and that was about all he understood about himself.

"I don't know if it's the pollen count or what," he told Nails, "but I hate the fucking spring. Sometimes I just wanna die in spring. What do I do next? Get a beeper or something?"

"You oughta get into chopping car parts or like the numbers or something," Nails said. Then they were silent.

Max emptied the gun and fired it at his temple. He grinned. Next thing he knew, Nails' keys were chiming. Nails was twisting locks in the hydraulic door. Next thing he knew, the elevator sunk listlessly. Max darted around his own past. He remembered a time his brother had sunk a hook shot at school without looking, from beyond the free throw line. He remembered an unfinished note his mother left for him one night—BE SURE TO. He remembered when he heard about Mike Maas and he wondered why he felt as though he were present at Mike's death. He could see it as clearly as if it were himself, and he had shown up in public flaming, hands outstretched.

Night swirled. When Nails let him out the main gate, he was stumbling and he couldn't remember a thing, couldn't remember what had happened inside. It was drizzling. The highways were empty. He felt great. Ghosts were the New Jersey state bird. He passed the beer distributor, the freight tracks, the decoplex film palace, and when he got to the place where he had locked his scooter, nothing remained but sprung springs and chain links scattered across the

pavement like viscera, across pavement that had buck-
led. In the stress lines there, in the cracks, yellowed
grass grew up in tiny, fierce clumps.

   Okay, it was spring and Alice was sitting on the front
step thinking about procreation, well, thinking about
the evidence of procreation. She was thinking about
these kids that spontaneously generated in Haledon,
and how they put some fear of obsolescence in her.
At the school nearby, that afternoon, in another futile
effort to control the kids, the teachers had arranged a
game of Capture the Flag, and now the kids were all
over the heights, on their own recognizances. She
watched them pushing things around, flexing their
clout.
   They called each other names like Flash, Stretcho,
Jewel, or names that were simply a jumble of numbers
and digits, like serial numbers or license plates. Once
you believed you recognized a pair, or a foursome, they
dropped out of sight. Their distinguishing marks were
always shifting, the aluminum baseball bat, the catch-
er's mask, the walkie talkie or pellet gun.
   Ten, eleven, twelve years old. They came out of
nowhere. They crossed out the l's in *public*. They had
all these uninformed opinions, staked whole friend-
ships on flimsy data, refused to speak to one another
one day and conspired the next. They rang doorbells
and ran, tripped the handicapped, snickered at the
word *love*. A lot like people in their twenties, in a way.
   Alice's house was on the playing board of this game
because someone had lifted the flags, or the flags had
disappeared, and when she went to sit on the front
step, to watch the clouds overhead, to smell the Colt
pistol factory which was upwind that afternoon, kids

were hidden everywhere behind shrubs or on the lower steps of basement entrances. Which side was winning was long since forgotten. Only some ritual of capture remained.

Alice's mother slept upstairs in her bedroom, where she had lain all day since returning from the hospital. The ride back was as still as a funeral procession. Mrs. Smail, who was heavily drugged, didn't respond to Alice's ministrations. But she was awake. She was fine. Her body was whole. Alice was thinking about prosthetic devices as she sat on the step. She was thinking about women in wheelchairs, women with artificial legs, women with ivory canes, colostomy bags, women with falsies. There was something she liked about it. Prosthesis was inevitable.

The kid coming across the lawn wore an Indian headdress fashioned from aquamarine construction paper. He had underlined each eye several times with an orange magic marker. He thumped an open palm over his mouth. Almost disinterestedly, he asked which side she was on.

Alice didn't know. She said nothing.

"I gotta tag you just in case," the kid said, "nothing against you, y'know."

"Will do," she said.

He wore an extra-large football jersey over torn blue jeans. Grass stains everywhere. In the hole over his left knee, a clotting wound was visible, fouled by dirt and gravel. As he sat on the step with Alice, he produced a stack of baseball cards from his pocket and absently flipped through them, looking for doubles.

The landscaping in the yard was falling into disarray, and it was going to get worse. Dandelions would erupt. Gypsy moths would find a safe haven. Hedges that had been pruned back into orderly topiary shapes would sprout strange growths. It occurred to Alice that the kids, this generation that needed to be watched over the shoulder, could come in handy here. She asked the boy if he had ever cut a lawn. She asked him if she could maybe pay him to care for the lawn for a couple of weeks.

Soon, a second one appeared from nowhere—maybe he was crouched behind a bush right in front of them. Z, he said his name was, although he was almost definitely Teddy Diserio, Cleo's little brother. Alice had known her back before Cleo had gone off to the city to model.

The first kid leapt up, according to freemasonic obligations, and the two of them walked over to the bank of forsythia. They conferred. Alice looked up at the blinds that covered her mother's bedroom windows. Asleep? She thought of Lane. How to begin a conversation with him.

"You're going to have to come with us," the first kid said when they came back. Z. stood behind, arms folded.

"Yeah," Z. said.

"Oh yeah?" Alice said.

"Yeah," the first kid shoved his hands into the pockets of his jeans.

Alice thought about it. She put thoughts of her mother out of her mind.

"Let me get some coffee and I'll go. You guys want some juice or something?"

"Beer?" said Z. The first kid nodded. "Got any beer?"

Dennis had given up painting. Out by the railroad tracks he gave it up once and for all. All morning he had thought about it: he had tried to stretch a canvas, to set up an easel, to look over the photographs of his model, Alice, but he could not do it. He'd gone instead to fix the shower head in his parents' bathroom. And when he had finished that, he had set out walking along the traintracks, where he was heaving stones at a *No Trespassing* sign nailed into a dead maple tree. He was worried that Alice was in love with his stepbrother. It wasn't exactly the word, but it was close.

In the distance, where the tracks curved around town, along its auricles and ventricles, in the distance by the propeller manufacturing plant, Dennis could make out three small figures moving awkwardly along the tracks. They stopped and started. They made immeasurable progress. They tried to balance on the rail for a time, and then fell off. Dennis stood in the briars that grew along the cement wall of Dykes Metallurgy and waited.

A train eased around the curve in the distance and wailed plaintively. Plainsong. As it passed, he targeted freight cars from where he hid. The stones vanished into the din of the train. The kids, because that's what they were, arrived in the midst of this solitary fury. The train was still passing, its tip and stern miles off in either direction. They were the kind of kids who wore their baseball caps backwards, who wore safari shorts and tube socks. Dennis emerged from the brush as though there were nothing to it.

"Yo," one of them said.

"Yo, yourself," said Dennis.

The first kid fingered the rim of his baseball cap, as though he were concealing pine tar there. He mumbled a question.

Dennis reached down for another handful of rocks. The thing about figures on the horizon was that Dennis always imagined them to be of great help or great harm. These figures of myth weren't supposed to be mediocre. He thought about hopping a freight train.

"Don't try anything, bud," said the kid with the baseball cap, "we got cuffs here and everything."

Sure enough, he had a pair of plastic handcuffs in the back pocket of his shorts. One cuff was fixed around his belt loop in back, and he had trouble getting it loose.

"Don't bug me, all right?" Dennis said. He told them to pick on someone their own size. Then he got thinking about the kids. You could take one of them out with one whack on the side of the head. But the kids saw everything. They were witness to all that happened in the neighborhood. And he got thinking about Lane, back at the house. He started to pump the kids for information.

Lane stood in the kitchen, trying to open individually wrapped pieces of cheese. He was rummaging in a drawer, looking for a knife. His mother was over visiting Mrs. Smail, and then to the market, and then to the day care center, and then to the league meeting. He was exhausting his mother and stepfather, and he knew it. They were trying to get out of the house more often. It was okay. He didn't want the cheese. He wanted the knife.

The doorbell rang.

Lane stood still. He heard children's voices. The uncomplicated optimism of their voices. He thought of the names of children's games, Blind Man's Bluff, Knockout, Squid, Stickball, Kick the Can, Sharks and Minnows. Games that predated the flintlock and the discovery of the Garden State and would be here long after, long after Lane came to whatever he was going to come to.

He was afraid to open the door. Out of nervousness, though, he found himself standing there, his hands on the locks.

"Who is it?"

"Me," a voice said. "Newspaper girl. Collecting."

Lane said nothing. The house was silent. The blinds were drawn. The grandfather clock on the landing had come to a halt.

"Collecting," the girl said firmly. Again.

And Lane gave in. He turned the locks. It was not out of politeness or curiosity, but out of degradation. Lane didn't have the money, had no idea where his mother kept money in the house, if she did at all, and he felt compelled to admit this to the newspaper girl.

Fecund sunshine. The girl was cute, and Lane noticed this in an abstract way. Her bright blond hair, the archipelago of freckles across the bridge of her nose. He leaned in against the doorframe. Children were all around the house, up and down the block. Spring blossoms.

"Huh?" she said. "Got the money?"

Lane shook his head.

"Somebody said," she said. "They told me this week. Your dad."

"Not my dad," Lane said.

"Well—" said the newspaper girl.

Lane shook his head firmly. He walked out onto the front step. The birds and flowers had a greeting card banality.

"I'm going to walk a little," he said.

"Huh?" she said. She cocked her hip and stuck a hand on it.

"Gonna give it a try," he said.

She said. "We could ride my bike together."

"It's so bright," he said.

The rusted three-speed was tipped against a rock out by the sidewalk. Kids knew about riding handlebars, Lane remembered, it was a right of passage. Riding on handlebars, heavy petting, shoplifting, stealing drinks and sleeping over. He reached the bike, walking with the deliberation of an elderly person. He hadn't decided one thing or another. Three more girls emerged from behind the flowering forsythia. Makeup smeared garishly across their faces.

"Lay off," the collecting girl said.

The three clustered around where Lane was organizing himself on the bike. He straddled it. She was about to hoist herself up.

"Did you tag him?" one of the girls said.

The collecting girl nodded. One of the others, a little Asian girl, stamped her feet.

And then Lane stepped back over the bike and let it clatter over onto its side. He brushed off his hands. He slipped out of the circle of girls, and he didn't look back. He walked over into the driveway. Clouds were moving in from the west. The girls stopped arguing. They stared. A police cruiser was passing slowly in the street. The sound of a train.

Lane shook his head. Then he started to run. Off into the street, he started to run, his lungs heaving painfully, his unused body reaching and stretching.

The station was a ruin. There was nowhere in Haledon where the trains stopped now. Bound with their great freight they headed elsewhere. No structure remained to memorialize the passengers of another time.

These were the waning years of Garden State industry. What was left of the station was a roofless, floorless gathering of three walls, hunks of concrete scattered around its interior. No windows, no benches, no plumbing, no wiring, no telegraph, no impenetrable security fencing.

It was late afternoon when Alice and her captors got off the bus out by Dykes Metallurgy and started across the empty lots. One boy was still carrying the ice cream cone Alice had bought for him. A florescent sherbet overflowed from it. The sun passed behind a massive bank of clouds. Cars worked their way up the side of the cliffs above the tracks. Alice had a cigarette in the pocket of her rumpled white dress shirt.

"Smoke?" she said.

The kids' eyes widened.

"You guys don't have the goods, know what I mean? You guys are years away from it."

They seemed to crumble. That was how it was with the kids though, Alice thought. Youth was wasted on them.

"I dunno," the one with the cone said.

"You pussy," Alice said. She mussed the hair on the top of his head. He just took it. He didn't say anything.

Dennis appeared from inside the remains of the train station, as they were rounding one wall. He was smoking, too, and drinking a tall boy.

"Hey," he said.

Alice's heart sank. She wanted to flee. The truth was she had sort of forgotten about him since the other day when he took her up to Lane's room. She figured the problem would solve itself. She didn't run, though. Instead, she hugged him. They walked around the side of the train station, picking their way around shattered bottles and bits of twisted aluminum. The kids Alice had brought trailed behind. The one with the cone veered off on his own. Inside the station a group of them tended a small fire with sticks, lengths of hose, and coat hangers.

"I thought I was out for a walk—" Alice said.

"I've been out here all afternoon," Dennis said. "Hey, uh, how's your—"

They were both jumpy. Alice didn't say anything.

"I heard about her from my stepbrother," Dennis said. "That's how I heard."

And then they were arguing. The word *stepbrother* did it. No big surprise. Alice unburdened her heart. Her rage was aphrodisiac. She loved it. She loved to insult him, to call him a plumber, to muddle him with arguments he had overlooked, subtleties he hadn't understood. She didn't stop there either. She reddened. She started way back at the beginning. All the little moments that had failed all the way along. They all came out.

So Dennis got scared. He started taking it all back.

"You aren't going to like break up or anything, are you?" He said. "You wouldn't just—."

Most of all, she hated him for not seeing the answer to this himself. "Well, I don't know," she said. "How could I? Maybe I will, maybe I won't. How the fuck do I know?"

In his features there was a combination of fierce bloodthirstiness and transcendent joy. Somehow she was pleasing him. She knew the right things to say were in this direction. Dennis hadn't seen yet that he was basically *a nice guy*. Only injustice got him going.

The kids were busy. They started by toasting their bits of inanimate material over the trash fire. The friction for them was like an acceptable dose of radiation. Where quarrels took place, the kids were perfectly at home. But soon they started to tire. They remembered familial obligations. Evening neared, and they drifted away.

Alice and Dennis were sprawled on a long flat chunk of cement. Dennis was toying with a jagged hunk of glass. Overhead, clouds.

"Now what?" Dennis said.

Alice nodded.

A kid with a cowlick and football jersey was solemnly carrying a flaming twig around the room.

"You guys are a pain in the ass," Dennis said.

"They told us to," the kid said, "the teachers—"

Lane remembered days of promise and talent. Or he thought he did. As he walked. The talent was not fully developed—it was an idle sort of raw talent—and Lane did not use it at his job at the patent law firm. But now and then the memory came back. He had lost the sense of smell, the muscles in his neck had tightened, cramped. But he remembered the promise he'd had then. That was what motivated memory, lost promise. There had been luncheons, luncheons where they schemed. How to get more, eliminate impediments. Who had influence? What to wear? Those days mulling over inventions, scouring the libraries. Okay, he hadn't exactly been good at it, but he'd been there. At one time he'd been the smartest kid within miles, but as an adult, he'd just faded away. Dead inside. Dead as you get.

He was on the edge of the heights, walking. Below, Paterson was a smouldering crater. Traffic had come to a standstill on one of the clover leaves. Traffic helicopters circled the skies like birds of prey. At any moment, they seemed ready to disgorge infantrymen.

The road down into Haledon was strewn with wreckage and trash. Burnt-out cars, burial mounds of shattered glass, flattened, indistinguishable bits of biology, torn pavement, potholes full of ominous black soup.

His heart rushed a little, as it did in the old days. He loved destruction. The freight train coming around the bend was his ticket to the world of fiendish industry. He could jump it. He could jump it, or he could wait for an hour for it to pass. It wailed and surged by, like a cinematic train, some hulking icon of the last century.

"I'm doing something wrong," Dennis said.

"What you're doing wrong," Alice said, "is thinking about it, thinking that you're doing something wrong. Don't cave in, that's my advice. No one can stand someone who caves in."

The ruin was empty now. Alice and Dennis were unchaperoned. The Capture the Flag game was a dreamy mirage. Never again, maybe, would the kids get anything together. They would plan things in high school and after; they would plan drunkenness and fornication with the premeditation of serial killers, but they'd never act in concert again. Soon they'd be looking over their own shoulders at the generations to follow.

Alice and Dennis shared a joint. Dennis had the last tall boy. The kids had drunk a few. Alice and Dennis had each had one.

"Besides, I'm the one who's fucked up," Alice said.

Dennis smiled wearily.

"I oughta know. It's all downhill now. There was that one summer with the band, and since then everything's fucked up."

Dennis exhaled and then hit on the joint again.

"Aren't you going to—"

"Fuck that. Town is dead anyway."

The light was failing. The fire was going out. They sat and watched.

"I want to fix things," Dennis said, "just tell me what to do."

He was getting animated again. The creases and lines in his ruddy face shifted back and forth with his haggard reasoning. He looked homely when he was needy.

"We're sitting here," he said, "it seems okay."

"Jesus," she said, "you're not listening. It's not fixable. Okay?"

Dennis flung the last of the joint from his fingers where it was about to burn, and it fell in amongst the slabs of cement.

"C'mon," he said. "We had some fun. Don't you want—"

"Nope," Alice said.

He paced in the ruins, now, picked his way through rubble and packaging. He told her his van was wrecked. It would never start again. They didn't make them like they used to. It was a halfhearted plea.

"Wait," Alice said.

Her hand was outstretched. She was waiting to be helped up. Nothing subtle about it. What changed her mind? It didn't matter what she thought, really. She could work him over, leave him feeling blue; she could get off. It would be easy. It was some modern, civilized idea about what was primitive. They flung themselves on a slab of concrete, kissing, fumbling. Something was falling out of the sky, rain or hail or ash or debris. Evening rallied around them. Alice groaned: she fabricated a groan. She was untangling her pants. They were all inside out. She held his head between her legs. He was like a wasp darting around down there. She was worried about someone seeing, but then she wasn't. Soon she hoped someone would see.

"Fuck it," she said. When his head started to come up, when it seemed he was going to take this advice literally, she forced him down again. "Fuck it."

A train was galloping past.

"More pot maybe," she said. "More something."

Dennis was mumbling to himself. Why? And a figure was walking along the tracks. Dennis had three fingers inside of her and was licking the side of her thigh, and she was waving to the guy, getting ready to shout something, to really curse from the bottom of her heart. Then she realized it was Lane. Lane was walking past. Alice reached down to try and push Dennis off, to try and cover herself. They were out in the open. Everything was all messed up. Then she just lay there. She felt dead inside. The world knew all her crimes.

Lane ran. Alice faked an orgasm. Dennis tugged at her in some regularized four-four rock and roll rhythm. He was jerking himself off. He wanted more. Did he see, and just ignore it? Later, she figured it out. He was trying to forget.

Through streets like dangerous waterways customized vehicles passed at a crawl with music thundering from the dashboards. The horns, useless in emergencies, played West of Network or Running Scared or Lost Your Lover or Shot Her Down. They were cars with petulant appetites, cars that required work. Spit and polished cars. Max Crick, on foot, in downtown Haledon heard the horns, heard their technological virtuosity, his pulse soaring from all the speed. It was raining.

He was thinking back on his own cars. He was remembering the sound of one of his cars running up on the median strip at the entrance to the tunnel. A horrible sound. One of those nights he was trying to get out of state. The humiliation of being on foot that time. On foot with a passenger, also on foot. It was that girl from that band. He'd mashed up the front end. Oil was leaking everywhere. They just walked away. It took a long time.

And here he was again. The rear ends of these luxury cars were inches from the ground. They were low riders. They passed down these streets with the majesty of cruise liners in an era of air travel.

No stars, as befitted evening in the Garden State. The nightlights of residences, the lights of wide screen television, were shrouded in a mild fog. Max settled down on the bench at the bus stop as though he were to occupy it for decades to come. His clothes were soaked through.

He had ignored the passersby, until he noticed the gait of one of them, the guy rounding the corner by the store marked CHECKS CASHED CIGARETTES. A nervous gait, a gait something like one of those dogs, retrievers, that seemed to run diagonally. All of Max's friends, or at least his friends from the past, dragged their feet—maybe everyone in Haledon did—but this shuffle was unmistakable.

The bus came then. With a sigh of disappointment its doors flapped open. The bus driver glared out at Max. But Max was looking at Lane.

"Was going to—" Lane said.

"Buddy," Max said, "Pal."

Lane stared. The bus driver gestured. In or out? The doors cluttered shut again. The bus was gone.

"Come stand under this streetlight, man. Let me look at your face. I wanna get a look at you."

Max led Lane and Lane said nothing. The shoulders where Max touched gave, were spongy. Lane's collar was not straight. He was unshaven. Max gazed into his features. The face was pale, troubled, disturbed by stresses and swellings of anxiety.

"What are you doing?" Lane said.

"Looking."

"Oh, Max. You wouldn't believe it. I'm—"

"I heard you were here. Your brother—"

Max figured that Lane was about to cry, that Lane was too old to cry, that Lane would not want to cry in front of an old friend. He responded honorably. He walked off. Ten paces off, he watched Lane shudder, as though it were nothing at all.

"They got drugs for what you got man," he called. He couldn't stop himself. "I'm telling you."

Lane's voice was husky. "That's maybe—oh fuck. My brains are all fucked up. I can't think—"

"Well, what do you want me to do about it?" Max walked methodically toward Lane. He offered him his soaked denim jacket. "I got some speed—"

"A ride," Lane said. "Can you help me get a ride back up—"

The rain began to fall harder. It was torrential. Rain that scorched holes in plants. Lane was hopeless. Max wanted him to get lost. Max wanted him in or out.

"Check cashing place," Lane mumbled. They fled.

"What are you doing back here, anyway?" Max said.

Lane shook his head. He shivered.

Max opened the door to CHECKS CASHED CIG-

ARETTES. From their spot in the doorway, he shouted at the guy behind the counter. "When's the next bus, friend?"

"Just left," the man said.

"This guy's sick," Max said. "My friend here he's sick and we gotta get him back up to the heights. You got a car we can use or anything?"

"No car."

"Max," Lane said.

Max waved him off. "Just shut up. I'm working here, all right?"

And then Max got the idea about the guys in the luxury cars. On the street. Max left Lane behind. He went out and waited for the tunes. He tried to wave them down. The first few passed, but at last one guy stopped, stopping all the traffic behind him, too. Max smiled, as the guy rolled down the window on the passenger side. Max pointed at the hunched figure in the doorway of CHECKS CASHED CIGARETTES.

"It'll only take like fifteen minutes," Max said. "And maybe I can make it worth your while."

"Forget about it," the guy said. He threw the car in park—cars lined up blocks back on Clinton sounding their orchestra of unrest—and stepped from it. He strode across the street as though he had just bench-pressed a phenomenal weight.

Max followed him to the doorway. The guy asked Lane where he was going, and Lane told him, and then the two of them organized him with reassurances. It would be okay to get in the car now. Nothing would happen to him.

"Ah, no, no." Lane whispered to himself.

The weightlifter and Max figured out it was turning into a battle of the wills, a use-of-force type of situation.

Lane was white as a sheet. Nothing doing. Cars lined Clinton. Must have been backed up for miles. But Lane wouldn't budge.

So they just grabbed him, just picked him up. The guy with the car was tough.

Max felt like a motherfucker when he slammed that car door, but it didn't last too long. His mind was already on other things. Like a place in Newark Bay where, at night, the water was low enough that the rats came out from where they were hidden. They clamored up onto the banks of the bay in waves. Max waved at the low rider as it carried Lane off, but he was already thinking about these other things. Waving and thinking.

4 /   Saturday night again. Louis Giolas—one-time guitarist of Haledon's Critical Ma$$—was waiting for the keg to arrive with the nervous excitement that always characterized the hours before a party.

Kickass roof party, kickass rock and roll roof party, paint the town red, April Fools, all that shit. And L.G. was thinking about sex again. Hopefully thinking. Unclad bodies, female bodies, in regrettable positions; partially clad female bodies, parts of these bodies in isolated consideration, an inch of thigh, a sliver of buttock; lips of women speaking vowels, women brushing back their hair, pubic hair, women in tight pants, in no pants, women, women.

L.G. had strong feelings about his own erections. And he had no control over his lust, or said he did not. Something about parties got him going this way, or something about waiting for parties. Fuck anything wanted to get fucked. Tap the keg. Simple as that.

Ideas blossomed in him like poisonous flowers. Bands from the area—D'Onofrio, The Null Set, The

Corinthians, Pontius Pilate. They would play like a stripped down kind of thing. The place overlooked the river, there was only the night shift at the shampoo factory. No neighbors to bother maybe. No cops. He had photocopied the invitation, handed it out at Ben Dover's, Bottled Blondes, at clubs in the next towns. Critical Ma$$ would be there sort of. In reconstituted form. Well, if Alice was going to come.

He borrowed the panel truck from the mall where he worked as a carpet salesman. He carted the P.A. from the musical rental place up to the top floor of the old factory. He did it slowly, precisely, by himself. The drizzle had let up. Just foggy now. The weather would hold maybe. The radio said dense fog in the evening. No problem—save money on a fog machine, on dry ice.

Where he stood, up on the roof, he could see them flattening cars and stacking them up like huge envelopes. A red compact car. An old Cadillac.

Once he had been to a party in Haledon where a guy had had his head blown off tapping a keg. The keg was like an ICBM. It must have gone up forty feet. The party ground to a halt after that, after Bobby got killed. There was a lot of blood. It was a big thing in Haledon. That and Mike Maas.

Actually, L.G. had not been out by the keg. He had been inside. He hadn't seen the blood. He had not seen Bobby; he had just seen what was left on the street. Come to think of it, Mike Maas had been there when Bobby had his head blown off. Mike had been down by the keg.

Anyway, L.G. was waiting for the truck to come with the beer, with the ancient nozzle and tapping apparatus that never felt the same to him since that night when the keg exploded.

Kickass rock and roll party.

Other things he had done at parties that he regretted included following Annie Sprain into the bathroom to do a few lines. Just sat right in her lap while she was trying to go to the john. Kissed her on the lips. He tried to hoist her skirt, he really did. She tried to throw him off. He got really mad, and she got mad, too. Annie slapped him. She removed a spike heel and went at him. She was trying to beat on him with the shoe, and, at the same time, she was trying to straighten things up. It couldn't work—how could it have?—and she sort of, well it was pretty fucked up her trying to get out. They fell out into the hall and she was weeping. That was the thing he never counted on, that she was going into the bathroom to take a leak. He was thinking about cocaine. Parties were supposed to be fun, but lots of times they weren't. People were always getting confused.

And there was a night some dance band from the city had rented out Ben Dover's and the place had been filled with guys wearing tuxedos and smoking jackets and stuff. Being a regular he got inside, even though his dress was not in style. For a while things were going okay, although he hated bands with too many keyboard players, but he hit that point where he had suddenly drunk too much. Plus, he didn't know anyone there, really. He was juggling syllables, trying to say them very slowly.

And then a guy at the bar remarked on his leather pants. This guy said he liked his pants. He kept saying it, about the pants, about how L.G. looked fine, really fine. And so L.G. broke a beer bottle over the guy's hand. It really gashed him pretty bad. There was a lot of blood. It really bothered everybody. They threw him out of the bar, and the last thing he saw on the way out was the guy clutching his hand.

Of course, he wouldn't do that now. He wouldn't break a bottle over a guy's hand. That was before the job as carpet salesman. Sad what will calm you down, L.G. thought, or maybe you just calm down no matter what.

And one night after a party he had tied a girl up. He had spent half an hour looking for something to tie her up with, after which she was pretty tired and irritated by the whole thing. He tied her up and then went out to watch television—maybe he watched pornographic cable television, he couldn't remember— but every time he went into the bedroom to look at her tied up—she was watching the digital clock turn over, listening to a cassette—he lost whatever interest he had. The thing about the pornographic cable stations was that all those commercials saying the program would be right back, those were really the best part. Like the best thing about a party is getting ready to go to it.

One night he convinced Scarlett to sleep with him. Scarlett from the band. They had been out late after playing at some bar. A good example of bad casual sex. The example being in persuasion. What made someone fall for all that stuff, unless they were made to fall for it from the beginning? Or else one day, like with Scarlett, the stars were lined up right or something, and it just happened. Scarlett just came around this night. She was in reduced circumstances, willing to do things. L.G. knew that people had to be in reduced circumstances to be at his house, and he just got used to it. The fact was a lot of people were there one time or another.

And a girl came with them. A young girl. Scarlett didn't talk him out of it, and this girl liked the idea. It was the best everyone could do right then.

On the roof, waiting for the kegs to come, waiting for the party, L.G. remembered how he couldn't concentrate. The numbers were all wrong. Both of the women were kissing him, each on a different cheek, or he was kissing one of them, and the other was as well. He never knew which way to turn. Or he would have his arms wrapped around Scarlett, and legs around the other girl, or one of the two of them was in this same position. Guys in finance could become accustomed to this kind of calculation, but not L.G.

It had nothing to do with girls sleeping with girls, the way L.G. saw it; it had to do with a man trying out this thing that had been on his mind only to realize that it wasn't on his mind anymore. Fantasies are like ideals: they're out there just to prevent dead reckoning. Close in on them and they move. Further out, mostly.

He felt with Scarlett and the girl that it would be impolite to get off, to come. Anyway, he normally managed that and slipped right away into unconsciousness. The worst possible scenario would be to wake to them going at it hours later. L.G. actually faked sleep to escape participation. Like at a slumber party of old, when the kids woke the parents and then drew their covers up over themselves. He feigned sleep, until the girl went off to the bathroom. Then he just couldn't resist going at it with Scarlett. The grass was greener. Well, what he was doing really was just sort of rubbing against her because he *hurt* down there from all this. He felt like a minnow stuck on the end of a fishhook. And Scarlett was looking away. Scarlett was off somewhere. She looked lonesome. And when he came on her hip—it just happened, nothing to it really—she started to cry.

L.G. begged her not to cry, because the girl was coming back and she was maybe sixteen. He begged her not to let the girl see. The least they could do— he was whispering—was to treat the girl right. She was just a kid. Scarlett wasn't having any of it. Scarlett bawled. It had been a shitty idea right from the start. It had been a drunken idea. Just people taking advantage of people. Dehumanization cubed. Three people getting what they thought they wanted and then not wanting it. Same old fucking story.

L.G. was already out of bed as Scarlett's speech was being directed at him. He was wiping himself off with a sock, as he went to find the girl in the bathroom where she was smoking a cigarette and, well, she was crying too. What could he say? He couldn't say anything.

And the truth was all this happened because of Alice. He really wanted Alice, not Scarlett, not some club girl. The night with Scarlett was really about Alice. Alice's cruelty, her meanness, these moved L.G. He even dreamt of her sometimes. Dreams in which she enumerated his failures, called him a shit, a hack, a sellout. These dreams galvanized his new life.

The two mothers were ensconced in the sick chamber. Ruthie, in the armchair, fumbled with a pair of dark glasses. She folded them, put them away, took them out again. The light coming in through venetian blinds was gray and dull. Evelyn Smail, bed-ridden, was a mound of pillows and knees. From time to time,

Ruthie rose to straighten, according to instincts that no longer comforted her. She gathered up a filmy expanse of nylons from just beneath the bed and set them on Evelyn's dresser. She plumped one of Evelyn's downy pillows.

"He's seeing this psychiatrist four times a week starting this week." Ruthie stood in the center of the room. "They settled on that at the first session. Four times a week. I'm going to say something about medication: I have been looking in the *P.D.R.* I know a thing or two."

Mrs. Smail nodded gravely.

"And that's on Monday. So we'll just make it through the weekend."

Ruthie disappeared into the bathroom where her voice rang amid the lively reverberation of those tiled surfaces. "You remember that fellow who lived down the block, whose daughter was so . . . You remember how horrible he looked—"

"What does your husband say?" Evelyn said.

"He's coming around. He believes more in some kind of bootstraps stuff, and he would advise Lane to get back to work. But even he can see that won't do any good now."

Ruthie sat on the edge of her bed.

"I've never been so worried," she said. "Well, but I came over here to see how you were doing."

"Oh, I don't want to talk about me," Evelyn said.

And Evelyn stirred. She lifted her legs from under the light summer blanket, smoothed down the pale blue nightgown which ballooned around her thighs— she was embarrassed at the sight of them—and slid to the edge of the bed.

"Are you getting up? Are you sure? Are you ready?"

"I've got to have a cup of coffee," Mrs. Smail said. "I've got to get up some time. The whole house is on remote control. I might get used to it."

Swaying, as she stood, Evelyn knew a kind of pride: the sort the handicapped must feel when they first roadraced in their chairs. A cup of coffee this day amounted to award-winning stuff. She was thankful for the shoelaces, for the venetian blinds, for all small accomplishments.

"Where's Alice?" Ruthie Francis said.

"She's skulking around someplace. Still in bed, probably."

"Hmm—"

"She's on her last days around here." Evelyn said.

They were in the corridor. Dust balls careened along the baseboards. The pale yellow walls were unadorned. A silent neglect permeated the house. At the top of the stairs, Evelyn concentrated on the banister, on getting ahold of it.

"I'm not going to stay either. It's too—"

The door by the top of the stairs, the door to Alice's bedroom, was open a crack, enough for Ruthie and Evelyn to notice. Black lingerie was clumped just inside the doorway.

"Three in the afternoon."

"They get over this," Ruthie said. "Everybody says."

Lane lowered himself into the bathtub. In this temperature—at the high edge of bearable—the heavy metals would be leached from his body. In the Northern countries where melancholy was prevalent, Lane thought, the sauna originated. The light was bad, and the citizenry drifted into truculent silences, until the hour of the sauna.

He filled his time with lists of desperate cures. Heliotherapy, hydrotherapy, vitamin therapy, abstinence.

Lane would try each. He feared the moment when he stepped out on to the bathmat. He feared the end of each reprieve.

Lane had balanced the plastic jar of tranquilizers on the edge of the tub, along with a glass of tomato juice, and now as before, the question was not of the feasibility or the logic of taking his own life, but of timing. Now or later?

He had to think things he didn't want to think. What he had seen in the train station, for example, had stuck in his head. Dennis tonguing Alice's thigh. The ridiculous thatch of pubic hair. The sheen of sweat on them both. The false smiles of erotic transportation. After, he hallucinated the smell of vagina on his own fingers, couldn't shake it, imagined it wreathing him as he undressed for his bath. And then he wondered why the smell no longer aroused him.

And he was troubled by the memory of the woman in the Empire State. They had argued on the fifth or sixth date. This time—he felt terrible about it. The conversation returned to him over and over. His response, which was no reponse at all, which was silence because he couldn't think of the right thing to say, could not think of anything to offer, had changed things for him.

And now he floated in murky water. His body seemed frail, tiny, breakable. Driftwood. Baby's breath. Everything was quiet. He opened the jar of tranquilizers, shook out a half dozen. Washed them down with his own bath water.

And he remembered how he lost his virginity in college. It was with a woman in his philosophy class, in freshman year. She was sullen, homely, fiercely opinionated in class. He had seen her, had tidied himself for classes on her behalf, without ever having even spoken to her. She was simply someone else preoccupied with philosophy, who argued persuasively against some things, against moralists, for example. Lane wondered if by now she had forgotten about all of it, or if she remembered with the detail that he did. Anyway, Lane had figured since she had presented a paper about the absence of inner lives, that she would do anything. He figured she had no shame.

Conversation was easy, it turned out, or conversation of a type. They were out at a bar, arguing about the possibility of alternate worlds. Real, honest to God possible worlds. And somewhere along the line he told her he wanted to go back to her apartment. He just blurted it out. She agreed. Agreeing didn't imply she was passionate about it, but she agreed anyway. Nothing mysterious. In a rare moment of playfulness, Lane stole her handbag as they were going out of the bar. The philosopher didn't chase him to retrieve it. She took no notice when, down the block, he opened it to examine its contents, and found it almost entirely empty. It contained only a wallet and keys.

Lane was drunk. When they got inside, he wasted no time. He hugged her to him, took off her glasses. They fell onto her carpet, halfway into an open closet. Discarded clothes served as their tattered coverings. It was the softest place. They did not kiss. He came right away. On her leg. It took a minute and a half, and then he was just lying there with this woman for whom love was a neurological event.

"I gotta go," Lane said. "There's something I have to do. Well, you know. I have to—"

She just rolled away. Didn't move or anything. Just lay there facing away, leaking him out onto a lavender cardigan sweater or an old plaid skirt.

"Give me your number," he said. "I'll call. I'll see you soon. In class."

What a relief when he realized she wouldn't honor the request. What a relief to be out of that room, though by the end of the week he began to plot the encore.

Ruthie started up the back stairs looking for him. It was the first thing she did when she came home now. She climbed the back stairs, and found the bathroom door closed. The sound of water. She went past, down the hall to his room, and straight to the bedside table where he was keeping the pills. The jar was gone.

Back at the bathroom door: "I'm back," she said. "What are you, uh, what are you doing?"

"What do you think?" His voice echoing on the tiled surfaces.

"How long have you been in there?"

He said nothing.

"What do you have in there with you?"

Her hand closed around the knob.

"What do you mean?" he said. "Tomato juice?"

Then some time passed while the two of them, on either side of the door, were still. In the water, Lane didn't move.

"Well, can I come in?" Ruthie said.

"No, please don't come in, okay? I'm not dressed or anything."

The towel was draped across the hamper, where he always left it. She heard him moving, reaching for the hamper, that old white hamper that had been there for more than a decade, and she imagined the look of him, there, dripping.

"I want to know how important it is that I don't come in," she said.

And then, since it wasn't locked anyway, she just shoved the door open.

Lane was trying to remove the plastic jar. Halfway across the bathroom, only several feet beyond the hamper, the trash barrel lay unemptied, and he had just set it on the top, on top of the toilet paper rolls, the plastic packaging, the abandoned razor blades he was trying to mash down the jar, bury it in garbage. And Ruthie went straight there, noticing only later how he clutched the towel around himself, how even then he was shy about his body—his concavities, his angles.

"What are you doing with these?"

"Taking one. What else would I do?" He looked down.

"One?"

"Sure," Lane said.

"One?"

"You don't—" he said.

"Tell me."

"Oh, Mom." He wanted to say something else, but he couldn't think. Ruthie listened. Nothing came.

In her arms, his dampness, his damp hair, his clammy, pale body. There wasn't much left of him. Right under everyone's eyes he had given out.

His hurried explanation, when it came, didn't make much sense. He didn't know, didn't know. He mumbled in fits and starts. Something terrible was going to happen, something really terrible.

Soothing words came to Ruthie. She called him sweetheart, darling, told him everything would be all right, all while she plotted phone calls, plotted avenues of advice and recourse. Categories from psychiatric texts, words and prescriptions, these routes, through traffic snarls, over bridges, through tunnels, to nearby hospitals, all this while pretending comfort.

Lane was shaking.

"I'm going to have to call the doctor. I will have to tell him. It doesn't make any sense otherwise, right?"

Lane nodded.

"How many did you take?" Ruthie said.

"Just six" he whispered.

"I'm not going to have to talk you around, keep you on your feet or anything, am I?"

Lane shook his head. "I just want to sleep one night all the way through."

"You aren't—" she said.

"Not enough," Lane said.

Alice's eyes were pincushions. Her eyes were Liquid Crystal Displays. Her flesh shone like synthetic fabrics. She was part rayon, part lycra, part orlon. She could feel each cell lost in the vanquished part of her head.

After her shower, she wrapped herself in a threadbare towel—it was left on the floor from the previous afternoon—and, pausing in the hall to light a cigarette, she headed back to her room. In spite of her discomfort—there was a way in which Alice cherished her hangovers—she felt ready for the day. Saturday was the best day of the week. It was after three. She had stayed up the night before by herself, drinking, and she had thought long and hard about it, well, actually she had made up her mind this minute. She realized she wanted to go to L.G.'s party. Maybe Scarlett would play a song with her. Maybe it would be something like old times. Why not? She was already back at Dover's.

In her room, she stopped to make her way through the pile of clothes in the middle of the floor. She was looking for the black leggings that were in there somewhere. Then, she saw. Then, she figured it out. Her mother and the gigantic trash bag. A trash bag the size of a car.

"What gives?" she said.

"A little cleaning," Evelyn said.

"Yeah, but you shouldn't be up—"

"My prerogative," Evelyn said.

She removed the birch branch from the middle of Alice's sculpture and stowed it in the bag. Alice was stunned. Her vinegary senses came to.

"Hey, get the fuck away from that."

Alice hiked the leggings up under the edge of her towel urgently. She let the towel drop to the floor.

"You're just going to pass out," she said, cigarette dangling from her mouth, "I'll have to search around for smelling salts and you'll be like lying in the middle of all this shit."

Mrs. Smail lifted the sculpture apart gingerly—the flatware, the condoms, the coathangers. It became a bare tree, a fossil. It was a chair overturned in the center of the carpet, nothing more.

"I think I'm going to sell," Alice's mother said. "So maybe you ought to think about getting a place for yourself."

To Alice, her mother was calm, unperturbed, nothing like the prone body in the hospital.

"I hope you do fucking pass out. I hope you fall down the fucking stairs passing out."

And she headed downstairs, one thing on her mind: Home Shopping Network.

* * *

Scarlett got ready for parties too early, arrived early, and then sat around by herself, plotting ways to leave. For the April Fool's Day party, she had spent a while dressing: black jeans, white tee shirt, and the black veil she wore for the occasion. But once she had settled on the outfit, she couldn't sit in her apartment any longer. On the loading dock in front of the building, she tried to decide whether to go in or not. For April Fool's Day she had affixed to her jacket a daisy—it squirted grape juice—and on the loading dock she tested it out. It arced outwards several feet, a limp stream. Ideal. She hoped Alice wanted to play, if they got a chance. Just a couple of old songs.

The door to the loading dock was propped open, and a piece of yellow legal paper was taped to it with black electrical tape. PARTY HERE. Scarlett made her way through empty corridors, up the staircases, taking pleasure in the echoes in the old place. It was a warehouse as still as a house of worship. Playing loud in a warehouse was the best. It made clear how rock and roll was a kind of religious music.

She hit the roof door and it careened back. L.G. was at the perimeter, over by the fire escape, staring out into the vastness of New Jersey. Paterson off to one side, and Nutley and Dint and Malagree. It was like some Netherlandish landscape, all light and air.

They smiled and hugged. Well, it was okay. There was awkwardness for a long time now. L.G. was dressed in the pink leather pants, a black satin shirt, and steel-toed cowboy boots. He had cut all his hair off, and it didn't go with the clothes at all. The clothes were leftover from another time. He had cut himself shaving too. A fleck of tissue still pocked his chin. He asked if she was going to wear the veil later.

"Where's the crowd?" Scarlett said.

"Coming, coming," he said, "you guys gonna play or what?"

There was a stack of guitar cases over by the tiny stage area. Five or six guitars, acoustic and electric. Monitors and microphones arranged in a semicircle. On the opposite side of the roof a small sound board had been erected.

"Everybody in town, man, everybody. We got guys from D'Onofrio, from Little Fishes, from Martial Appetite. Biggest gathering of talent in a long while. In a long time."

They stood by the guitars—stacked like cord wood—and then they moved to the edge of the roof again. Nothing to say. The husk of a burnt building lay below. Beyond it the Dern River ebbed along its course.

"We could play somebody else's guitar, right?" Scarlett said, "I mean, I don't know if she's—"

L.G. grunted.

"Listen," Scarlett went on, "I'm going to walk around for a while."

He didn't say anything.

She stood at the door.

Maybe the whole party was an April Fool's joke, some kind of April Fool's coercion by L.G. Maybe it was some kind of April Fool's restitution.

Dennis and Max cruised the Pulaski Skyway. They hit the road with a bunch of tapes of bands long since disbanded. Dennis had lost the keys to the van somewhere, so Max had yanked the starter out, and now there were loose wires hanging out of the dash. Max could do stuff like that—hot wire.

Clouds blackened the sky, but they were the highest of clouds, and the weather held for the time being.

The Newark Bay glistened spectrally. Max chattered about this base, this was the best base in the tri-state area. It was almost patriotic to smoke it. It would help with the debt thing, the South American debt thing. It would help them honor their loans.

"The easement of it, man," Max said. He lit the pipe. "Go faster."

They circled around the snarl on the approach ramp again, where this car was overturned. Traffic slowed; Max and Dennis watched the emergency personnel the way others evaluated an athletic performance. Then they took the exit past the refineries, through the rushes, and then back around again past the overturned car. The ambulance had already gone. There was no human element to the drama. To Max it was just pastiche, tableau, landscape, colorfield.

He babbled about the music scene. He wasn't listening to anything new; he was all in the past now; the great bands confined themselves to just a few good records; the great records best dealt with one subject and that subject was sex.

But he was the type, Max went on, who was early to parties. He was early even when he planned to be late. He planned to be a half hour or forty-five minutes late when everyone else was planning to be much later still.

"What is your brother doing? Is he coming to the party or what?"

Dennis changed lanes, exited. They took the cloverleaf so fast the back of the van was rattling, and Max slid centrifugally against Dennis. "Fuck if I know."

"Here, try this, all right?"

It was hard to tell which was the van thundering with velocity and which was the tape deck turned up. A kind of metal sludge. The Pulaski Skyway rose off to one side, now, a scorched land bridge, and they descended into an area of heavy manufacturing. The nuclear reactors rose over the highway like vast public monuments, public shrines. Max lit the ether to oxidize the drug. The traffic became ensnarled again, but this time there was no accident, only the sobering beauty of the Garden State itself—the evening light, the search lamps that passed through its skies, the dirigibles with their trade messages, the steam pouring from the reactors.

The drums were all there was to that song. Max was onto lasers now, how he'd been out repairing this cable hookup late one afternoon last winter, how this woman's television set kept picking up the police band, how he had set the parts out on a series of rags on the floor, how when he went out to the truck to relax for a minute, smoke a joint, he had looked up and there were these green lasers, four dividing into eight, eight into sixteen, criss-crossing the sky. They quivered and shook. Rattled and shimmied.

Well, first thing was he thought he was making it all up. Some kind of withdrawal, maybe, due to the inadvisability of going hours at a time without real substance abuse. He lit the joint and it still didn't go away, and so he knocked on the woman's door, and told her to come on out. It was nuclear annihilation, was what he told her, only seconds left for that last moment of human contact. She laughed. They repaired to the porch for a drink.

Max and the woman toasted. It was right around rush hour. It was the dead of winter. Calm. The lasers squiggled. Sort of how he imagined seeing the Northern Lights would be, except better, more dependable, because you could have quality control in this case. The woman was wearing a robe now, it was riding up.

They were sprawled on the Indian rug. He could see her undergarments. She was staring up at those lasers, but she was smiling about her undergarments.

Max hugged the first hug like he was blowtorching winter—this was what he said—but the second hug lacked that same, you know, whatever. The second hug had a lot of deadness in it. It all took fifteen minutes and in the middle somewhere the lasers stopped. That was when the woman really lost interest. She stopped moving altogether. He may as well have been involved with a petri dish. She sighed and rearranged herself.

"And then I found out later that it was like the sound check for this show at the racetrack. This rock and roll show. They were like checking out the lasers before the show to make sure they all worked."

"Jesus," Dennis said, "you're making all this shit up."

"Burned out, man," Max said, "totally burned out."

And Dennis told Max about one time he had seen these people out fucking by the railroad tracks, just fucking right out there in the rubble. Unbelievable.

Max set the pipe on the floor of the van. They eased up against the bumper ahead of them, and the car behind eased up on them. Things slowing down everywhere.

Really loud but L.G. was yelling something in Dennis' ear—when they got there finally—about a band sounded like The World and Its Mistress although it wasn't much of a name. Dennis and Max were climbing the stairs—L.G. just ahead of them supervising the transportation of another keg—and Dennis was remembering the guy who got it in the head tapping one once. The music was loud especially for acoustic stuff. It was loud down the block. The only sound, the only lights on this side of town were lights and sound that L.G. had provided. L.G. ruled.

And he smelled like beer, shouting in Dennis' ear, and he had that glazed look, that look of exertion, that people got from mixing drink and cocaine. Dennis probably had it himself.

L.G. kept shaking his head. And then Dennis got it—something to do with Alice. The World and Its Mistress was Scarlett and Alice. They were going to play.

The guys with the keg were stalled trying to get it around a banister.

"Jesus Fucking Christ," L.G. shouted, "it's gonna be like this all night. Back and forth. Gotta get some-body else next time."

Max was shouting behind him. Excellent, fucking excellent. Excellent fucking night, excellent fucking April Fool's. Fucking excellent.

The Poles were in from Bayonne, along with Eleven Jewish Korean War Veterans, Films Par Excellence, and the Catlips from Ridgewood, and Those Guys Who Strangled Their Wives, and Associated Traction, and Chrome; The Smirkes; Consuela, Gloria, Judy or June (all the way from Sparta), and another band called the Baedeker Girls, and the Hammerheads, the Leeches, the Fishguards who were really a splinter faction from the Voltaires and had the keyboard guy from Three Days in the Penitentiary playing harmonica for the evening—Max yelled continuously at Dennis, as they made their first pass around the roof—and then there was a girl who wanted to do folk songs who had once been the manager of Soldier of Fortune, and there was a real loser who had been like a roady for Gulping First

Drinks, and a pair of speed metal bands, Terminello and the Valkyrie. Those guys from D'Onofrio were there. The girls from Critical Ma$$. Only Nick the drummer was missing.

What Max was saying was that every rock and roll band in this whole half of the Garden State was at L.G.'s party. Well, not every one, but most of them were there. Max was gesticulating. There were more rock and roll people there than civilians. No one was listening to the music, though.

Some guy in leather pants and a tank top was sitting on a stool at one end of the roof—a couple of clamp lights were trained on him—and it seemed like he was tuning his acoustic guitar for fifteen minutes. Dennis had finished a cup of beer that was four inches of foam, and he and Max were back in line. They ran into Scarlett there. Everybody was in line. Everybody was drinking.

"We got caught in traffic," Max said. "We were out by the racetrack. Traffic all the fuck the way back to the beginning of time."

Scarlett and Max bantered about feeble acoustic versions of West of Network. Everybody was doing them. A pair of guys in the line for beer looked like they had just come in off the street, the one guy was wearing a button-down shirt and a baseball cap. He was neatly shaved and trimmed and combed. There was something about the whole thing, the whole party. And Dennis didn't want to talk to Scarlett anyway. He liked her and everything, but he just didn't want to talk.

"Alice drinking anything?" he said though, and Scarlett stopped in the middle of a sentence. "I mean I was just wondering."

"It's a casual thing," Scarlett said. "We're only doing two songs. It's acoustic—"

"Chill, man," Max said, "chill. We'll take a walk around the block or something, Jesus Christ."

"Nobody's gonna be able to play or anything," Dennis said. "That's the only reason I bring it up. She'll be so messed up."

Scarlett frowned.

The guys in front of them had filled four or five cups with beer, and now a long line wound back toward the stage. The music twanged shrilly. It was those same three West of Network chords they were always playing, and no one was listening.

The April Fool's party didn't have a single joke that L.G. could see. No traditional bad joke stuff, you know the rubber facsimiles of this and that available from the unnamed novelty shops of Fleece, N.J. Scarlett had a plastic squirting lapel flower earlier, and a veil, but she wasn't wearing them now. No one had called the cops yet. It was a big success. Maybe someone could come dressed as cops. Someone could say the cops were coming when in fact they were not. Or when they were.

Parties have a middle portion, between when everyone is nervous at the beginning and where everyone is passed out at the end. In the middle of the April Fool's party, everyone started to move downstairs into the building, into corners, into corridors. The music droned distantly. When one of the microphones broke down, L.G. just let it sit for a while. It relieved the audience of the burden. Anyway, it was just Country and Western. Everyone had a C&W song that they were playing that night. Everyone had something they didn't care too much about.

L.G. himself had other things on his mind. He had a real ballad in mind. A torch song. It was something he was working on. Something, when he recorded it, that was going to need string accompaniment. It was a sort of a hymn about betrayal. Critical Ma$$ really was this thing that was wedded to the time at which it was first formed. Finally L.G.'s songs were moving again. He was flux. The old ones would never sound the same. Nowadays you had to learn how to hammer on the fretboard, to use effects pedals like a son of a bitch. But the joke was he wasn't going to play tonight anyway. He was saving this stuff for just the right moment.

So he was checking on a couple of packages of plastic cups he had left in the janitor's closet on the third floor, when he found Alice in the stairwell, sitting alone. She looked great like that.

"Hey, I didn't even think you were gonna be here." His voice seemed to loud to him, but he just blundered on. He sat down beside her. "I mean, it's great you guys are here, you and Scarlett, and like you're gonna play and everything, right?"

But Alice had her face in her hands. You couldn't miss it. She had black fingernail polish on. He didn't know what to do, whether to offer comfort or what.

"I don't give a shit about that," she said. She didn't uncover her face. L.G. noticed her roots were growing out. L.G. mumbled that if there was anything he could do—

Alice asked if he had any drugs.

L.G. shook his head.

"You could get me a beer."

"I'll get you a beer if you tell me what's wrong."

Alice groaned. "What the fuck do you think? How

the fuck do I know? Life is wrong. Like men and work and health and real estate are all fucking wrong."

L.G. didn't say anything.

"Fuck you, if you think it's a joke."

"Look, don't take it hard," L.G. said. "Things will lighten up later. I swear." He stood up, bearing the stacks of paper cups above him as though they were religious chalices. "Hey, you know Bottled Blondes is closing down? Or changing hands or something. No more live music. It's gonna be like an oldies joint or something. Like wet tee shirt contests and stuff."

He started to trudge up the stairs again.

"Not that I got anything against wet tee shirts, you understand," he said. "I just hate things closing down. And people moving away."

Back upstairs, he got caught mingling. He mingled with all the old Haledon crowd. There were badass guys who worked in the service stations or like for the fire department. Badass guys. Guys who would drive in reverse at high speeds on foggy nights on the main roads. They were all here.

None of the guys on the stage, the ones who were still trying to play without amplifiers or microphones, none of them brought up the April Fool's thing. He stepped over the monitors as he was thinking this, when this band called Wandering Rocks, who were basically the old Fishguards (everyone was basically just from one or two bands that went way back—these bands that were like the Indo-European language of Haledon rock and roll), and as they finished a bluesy something with a bluesy sixth chord, he grabbed a guitar from on top of the stack by one of the amps.

"Hey, let's do West of Network, old time's sake, all that shit."

"Save it, man," said Harry from the Fishguards,

"leave it 'til later. We can do something else. Some cover or something."

Then the heavens gave out. Torrents.

Max and Dennis were rooting around on the third floor. The doors to the offices, all vacated, swung wide, and in each room they circled around absently. Trespassing as a kind of ownership. It felt good. Max carried two beers. Dennis carried two beers. They were talking about how there was nothing going on.

"The party had promise," Max was saying. "I was looking forward to this thing. It had promise and now there's nothing. Man. I can see that it's shit. The rain. You can't play live music in the rain. It's bullshit."

"It's only like eleven-thirty, Max."

"But you can tell. You can tell."

They went into the office marked Mooney Mail Order and slumped to the floor against the exposed brick walls.

Dennis asked if Max was holding anymore.

"I have like one joint, but I know where we can get more."

"How far?"

"Into Paterson."

"Where?"

"We could go to DD's," Max said. "We could cop there."

They lapsed into silence.

The corridors a shade of charcoal, all but emptied of light, as somber as mausoleums. Scarlett and Alice traipsed from door to door on the second floor; in each room they found a small splinter party. The storm had blasted the audience all over the premises. Now, in rooms emptied of furniture, where the service economy had created its backwater of small unimposing businesses, people in their twenties who couldn't find jobs even in an expanding economy, ran through unfinished verses of the same old songs, to drunken accompaniment.

Nothing as timid as acoustic guitars after you have played electric for a while. Like using a bayonet against an army with submachine guns, Alice thought. The sound of that lonesome strumming of open chords—that sound that immediately brings to mind campfires—it's so pathetic because it's so near to silence. As Alice and Scarlett passed from room to room they each made vows to themselves about their futures as musicians. They vowed never to play acoustic. They vowed never to go solo. They vowed never to play again.

Scarlett had a joint, and they were just looking for one empty room on the whole second floor to smoke it in, a room without a girl in it giving a blowjob to somebody. These things were on Alice's mind. There was something about fucking. Fucking was out of favor. It was an era of barter, or blowjobs and handjobs and stuff. Guys would try anything to avoid fucking. They would persuade you to accept ropes or shackles at the bedposts, while they went to masturbate in the other room, or they would want you to masturbate in front of them, or they would want you to pose for photographs, or they would want you to submit to mild cruelties, or to shave yourself in front of them, or to put things in yourself. And all because they were afraid to look you in the eyes and say you were pretty swell.

"Let's just sit in the stairwell," Scarlett was saying.

"I was already here," Alice said. They sat there anyway. "Don't you want to get out of here. This is fucking ridiculous. What time is it?"

"Like midnight or so," Scarlett said.

"Did they get the guitars out of the rain?"

And footsteps padded up the stairs. It was L.G. and Max and Dennis. They were wet. All three soaked through.

Max was wired again. He blurted out a paragraph of something about rain and going around the block—

"Yeah," Scarlett said.

"We got this idea," Dennis said.

"Yeah, yeah," Max said.

Scarlett smiled. L.G. smiled. Everyone smiled, though there was nothing much to smile about.

"Let's go for a drive," Max said. "Dennis has the van right downstairs. Let's go cruise the town. It's really been you know a while since we all did it. Since we were all in one spot."

"Three weeks?" Alice said. She leaned over the banister and looked upwards at the redundancy of stairs.

Scarlett asked about the party. What would happen to the party?

L.G. just laughed. "The party will take care of itself. Can't sift through the fucking wreckage until daybreak anyway. One fucking spin around the fucking block."

Gingerly he set his empty paper cup upside down on the stair. With his boots he crushed it.

"Yeah, let's cruise the city at low speed with the back of the van open, tunes up loud all that stuff," Max said.

Alice noticed that Dennis' voice didn't get raised in all this planning. She could see he didn't like any of it. In the silence right then, the five of them standing there, Max and L.G. were passing a joint, the sound of an acoustic guitar somewhere—badly in need of tuning—in this lapse when it felt as though nothing had happened, when everything was just the way it had been for a decade, Alice slid down three steps to where Dennis stood. It just seemed right. He looked okay. She didn't want to lead him on, but she didn't necessarily want him out of the picture either. It was one of those moments when a trivial question bore a lot of weight.

"What do you think?"

And it was a kind of trick question too: if he answered that he didn't want to go, that meant that he didn't want to see her ever again, and if he answered that he did want to go, well then that was an act of cowardice, because the two of them shouldn't have been in the midst of this crowd from the past, anyway. They should have been alone. And fuck all these other things, these schemes that were never going to materialize.

"Whatever you want," Dennis said. "I don't really give a shit."

She was surprised. And then she was pissed off. And then Alice grabbed his cheek with her hand—her nails were polished in black—and pinched it lightly.

"So cute," she said. Meaning he would never see her again. Signifying from now on he was as good as dead.

When L.G. came out the front door later, and they were all waiting for him by the van, it was like he was leaving a burning building. People were sprawled everywhere, he said, on the floor, in eddies of accumulated dust, in every room in the building. That was it, the big April Fool's joke, he said, that it was just a party, not some elaborate mating ritual. L.G. roared.

He threw back his head and bellowed. Easter Sunday had come. It was one in the morning. Christ pushed the rock from in front of his tomb.

The rain was coming down heavily now, with a somber intensity. The streets were empty, strewn with shattered glass, lined with bare trees. Dennis unlocked the back of the van, and Scarlett—ensconced totally in some mute period—climbed in the back with Max. He let L.G. in through the side panel. Alice sat in the passenger seat.

Max asked him to put the tape on before they had even started the van. Everyone knew that the trip wasn't going to live up to expectations. It was too late for speed metal, but Max played speed metal anyway.

They hit the streets of Haledon at eight miles an hour. The back of the van was open, and a moist April breeze played across them. Dennis headed down the road toward Paterson. They passed the strip joints, the fast food franchises, the Colt factory, the monumental Krakatoa factory. Music rumbled in the tape player. They ran alongside the river, and then back up into the heights. There was no conversation. At a crawl, Dennis eased past the Smail's place.

"Drive-by," Max said from the back of the car, "drive-by shooting."

"She's throwing me out," Alice said. "Did I tell you? She told me I have to get out."

Dennis slowed the van to a halt. The engine idled.

"Not like I'm heartbroken at this late date," she said. Then: "We should take them back. They're asleep, so let's just take 'em back."

"Where does L.G. live now?"

"An apartment over by the station," Alice said.

"We'll take him and then her and then we'll take Max up into the hills," Dennis said.

"Whatever you want," Alice said. "I don't really give a shit. No wait, let's take her up first."

"Why?"

"It's nearer. It's right down the hill."

Later, they pulled up in front of the exterminator's place, in the bus stop. Enmity had settled over the van. No one spoke. Alice was as awake as she had ever been, now, restive and disappointed. When Dennis roused L.G. to help carry Scarlett up the stairs, Alice offered no assistance. Nobody asked her anyway. Max, too, ignored the whole thing. She stared out the window on the passenger side.

"Woman at the cash machine, Max," she said, "she's out at the cash machine, on foot, on a Saturday night at two in the morning. What the fuck? Why bother?"

Max eased around the boxes of tools and the oxygen tank in the back of the truck, up into the driver's seat.

"A date," Max said, "what else? It's Saturday night. Or maybe like she's getting back from some total nightmare of a date."

And that was what gave her the idea. She was thinking, and then it came to her.

"Hey, you can drive a van, right?"

Well, Max could drive anything, of course. So Alice proposed it.

"So let's go get Lane."

Max thought.

"You want to just leave them there?"

Alice looked up at Scarlett's window, where the lights had gone on.

"April Fool's and all. It's not such a long walk—"

Max said, "You have a sick heart."

Max asked if there was any more beer. She handed him her cup of foamy dregs. Max smiled, and Alice noticed his teeth were all dead, all cemented in. From when he'd broken his jaw. There was an especially low form of bankruptcy in his smile. He drained the beer. He reached for the ignition. No keys.

So she got out, slammed the door, walked with the purposeful walk of the hardened criminal to the intercom of Scarlett's apartment, and buzzed. L.G.'s distorted voice replied. Alice told him to put Dennis on.

"We want to go and get some coffee at the donut place. Throw the keys down," she said.

"We're almost done."

"We'll get some coffee and bring it back."

He didn't answer, and she waited, staring at the stupid piece of plastic on the wall beside the stupid exterminator's place, thinking all the while that he knew too, that he had to know what she was about to do, and that it was all okay, hunky-dory now. When the keys fell, bounced once lifelessly, bounced again, she didn't look up. She grabbed them and ran.

Lane paced.

The night was not quiet. The drugs hadn't done anything. It was a facet of his parching solitude that he was always up now in the early morning. He fell asleep at nine in the evening from the tranquilizers and slept until two-thirty and then he lapsed into hysterical brooding. Sleeplessness that was more like waking dreams. He thought about humiliation. He remembered things. He made things up.

This time it was about how there was nothing masculine about him. He remembered a time when he had been okay at some of the things that passed for masculinity: inarticulate bravado, facility with sports and power tools, concealment of the emotions. Now, bed-ridden for no reason other than disinclination, he could see that anything masculine about him had vanished.

In fact, at 2:00, Lane decided he was really a woman.

It was worse than this. At 2:00, he had taken off his shirt to study his torso in the mirror. He became convinced that his nipples were like the nipples of a woman. Well, like the nipples he glimpsed as a boy when he woke one night and saw his mother wandering the halls of the house disrobed. His chest lacked hair of any kind, and his pectorals sagged slightly like a woman's breasts. His nipples were just like his mother's.

He dropped his boxer shorts to examine himself. His penis was the same little knob of lifelessness it had been for weeks now, but he took a new interest in an area just to one side there where he had often sprouted a rash years ago. There was a bunching there, a raw red line of perspiration and befoulment. This was it, he decided, alone at that miserable hour, this was his vagina, his uncompleted womanhood.

Lane collapsed onto the carpet, not believing, but not able to let up thinking.

He got up, went back to the mirror. He didn't want to look, but he did. He turned so that he faced away, and craned his neck, to examine his ass. His ass was pear-shaped. Not the square ass he associated with male youth, but a round voluptuous girl's ass.

He pulled up his shorts and hobbled across the room and onto his bed, shuddering. Down the hall, a noise at the window at the top of the stairs—the scrape of wood on wood. Lane wept.

A dim light in his room—she could see it as they slithered noiselessly through the open window, down the corridor. When they got to the door, though, she was struck with a sudden faintheartedness. Where was his family? Why could they just walk in like this?

She whispered to Max, "You're going to do the talking, right?"

"Don't sweat it—"

And then the door swung back, and the room leaked its halfhearted light into the corridor, and she could see his body stretched out, half on the bed, half off, his head covered in a tangle of bedclothes. It didn't look good.

Alice said hello.

From beneath the pillow Lane asked what they wanted.

"To see you, man," Max blurted out as though his teeth were chattering, as though it chilled him to be near the guy. "Just to hang with you, pal."

"I just—" he said.

"Come on out—" Alice said. "I can't fucking talk to you if you—"

His eyes were swollen, as he unwound the sheet from his skull; his dark hair was matted around his forehead.

Alice thought he looked pretty cute.

"What are you doing awake?" she said.

Lane shrugged.

In the doorway, Max was licking a joint. Alice sat on the stool by the bookshelves.

"Okay if I light this thing here?"

"Come on," Lane said, "you know it messes me up. I'm not feeling too great and that stuff, well, you've seen it, right? You've seen me on that stuff."

"Forget it, man, you have turned into a real drag, you know it. Anyway, that was like one fucking day.

If your head wasn't so loaded down with bullshit, you'd do fine with it."

Max put the joint back in the breast pocket of his denim jacket.

"You know what you need," Alice said, smiling this smile of good-natured concern. "What you need is a drink, Lane. You need to go out for a drink, feel the wind coming through the car window on the way to the bar, throw a couple of beers back, talk some trash, and throw a couple more beers back. You need to relax, take the plunge."

"That's right, man," Max said. "That's the truth."

He lay there without saying anything. It was like they weren't really there at all. Alice regretted the whole thing.

"You got some real clothes, Lane?" she said. "You got some clothes in the closet here?"

Max made himself useful. He headed for the closet and began rummaging through it—"Jesus, this shit must be ten years old"—yanking hangers out and piling things up on the floor of the closet. Finally, he emerged with a pair of khaki trousers and an old black turtleneck. "Here you go, pal. Let's get 'em on."

The trousers landed on him, and he didn't flinch, or turn his face away, or remove them to one side.

"What do you guys want?" he said. "I don't want to go anywhere. Please."

"Loosen up some," Alice said, "and that energy will come right on back. It really will."

Alice smiled plaintively. She could see that he didn't have any idea what to do, that he was trying to *guess* what to do, and that was how she knew he would come.

"Well, what's the plan?" he said. "Force? I just can't—"

THE

MONTH

OF

MAY

5 / When Lane got back on the first of the month, the orderlies took him back to the examination room and gave him a body search and a supervised urine test. It was his first trip off the premises and it reminded him of the day he came in. They gave him a scar search that day. And there had been a Q and A thing during the admitting interview. Lane had successfully named the presidents all the way back to the New Deal. He had done the nines table without a hitch. The New Deal, the Great Society, the Teapot Dome Scandal, Garfield and McKinley—Lane named a lot of things. It was some desperate performance. When the admitting doctor, a young guy in jeans and a pullover sweater, had asked Lane what brought him to the Motel, he'd said that he had always wanted to see Short Hills. That was the first thing he got right in the Motel: gallows humor.

First of the month, Earl the orderly received his jar of urine—as though it were some ancient anthropological artifact—and set it aside. He told Lane to wait for a minute, that the night nurse wanted to talk with him.

It was so rare that you were alone. He could have emptied out his urine, but now after three weeks they trusted Lane. So he occupied himself. He handled the instruments that were lying around. He had learned to take his own blood pressure in the Motel, because it was a place where they were always monitoring you, and that night, before Linda the night nurse came in, Lane took his blood pressure again. He was young and healthy.

The lunch with his mother—what about it? They were permitted to dine at the steak house in Short Hills, the one up the street. She'd parked the car right out front, so he didn't get to see much of the outdoors. And the conversation with Ruthie never got off the ground. That he spoke lovingly of guys like Eddie, who was inside after having taken seventy hits of acid in one day, who spoke in alliteration, this stuff seemed hard for her. She should have seen the novelty of his speaking lovingly of anything. Lane worried about Monday, when they both would have to see the family therapist.

Linda moved laboriously, through the door, with the certainty that she brought to the Motel, to its tasks— like sedating the guy who had come in strapped down the day before. She was obese. Her eyes were the color of slate. Lane had learned to trust her, or maybe he just trusted her first and learned about it later. But as she came to the examining table, where he was sitting, he felt okay.

"A couple of things happened while you were out today," Linda said. "I thought I'd fill you in, so you didn't hear it in a watered down version."

Lane nodded.

And then she told him about J.D., a girl on the ward, a woman he liked. A friend. Mortality was routine there, and everyone belittled it with practical concerns, but the staff also tried to get a lesson out of it when they could.

"Some stiches in either wrist, is all," Linda added, "and she'll be on some medication tonight. We asked her husband to take the ashtray out of her room last week, but he forgot. She broke the ashtray and used a piece of it."

The sensation of it was clear to him—the wrists were nothing more than the narrowest twigs on a sapling. It would be as easy as peeling a twig.

"You could try to talk to her later if she is awake and she's willing. It's best to get it out in the open."

Lane nodded again.

Linda asked if he had any idea, if he knew why she would have done it. Lane remembered seeing her come out of her room earlier in the week, rushing out of her room as though it were aflame, pitching herself in the arms of an orderly. Sobbing.

He shook his head.

Linda slowly bore herself up from the stool by the examining table. She put one enormous hand upon him, on his thigh. "Guess you weren't expecting to come back to this." And then at the door: "We did a room search, too, looking for sharp objects. Just to clean the place out. Your room was clean."

Lane nodded.

Then she said, "Are you okay? How was the lunch?"

The third day there he had wept and hugged Linda like a little kid, because of how low he felt, to be here in the Motel, to be playing volleyball in the gym, with a fractured wrist, with these misfits. They had no radios in the Motel, except in the gym, and that afternoon Devil on the Devil Train had come on the radio. He had headed back to his room. Linda came and talked to him. He wept. He hugged her.

Since then he had come up with some rules that governed the Motel. Since the third day he'd been thinking about it. First rule was everyone came in believing they didn't belong there. On the fourth day, after they'd been kept up a couple of nights being observed by the orderlies, everyone got a glimpse of what kind of shape they were in. On the fifth day, they set about disproving their diagnosis.

2) The main difference between the Motel and any other kind of institutional housing was its famous windows and doors. All the doors locked (except in the bedrooms); all the windows opened three inches only. Strict rules of ingress and egress.

3) No sharp edges: it had nothing to do with harm to the self (like J.D. proved, you could always figure a way). It had to do with sharpness in general. In the Motel, nothing sharp. Everything was free of that kind of keenness. Everything was regimented casually, calmly, totally.

Back to J.D. She had fallen apart on the job, her first day as a schoolteacher. This was the story on her, inside. She had been a bank teller for a long time, for years, and then she had risked upsetting things a little and decided instead that she always wanted to be a teacher. She endured the years of teacher's college, passed through a period as an assistant, all in preparation for that first day, the day she came down with hysterical aphasia. As she stood before her students, her mouth was frozen in a grimace of horror. She knew what was happening: it was as predictable as a stutter.

Tears came from her eyes. They led her out of the class. Other teachers actually had to help her from the room, and when she left it was for the last time.

Everyone in the Motel had a story like this. There was Elena, who had spent her adult life taking care of her spinster mother, until her death. After, Elena had lived for six months in her mother's bedroom, Lane had heard, without ever going outside. She had fallen into neglect. There was a guy, Anton, a weight-lifter and compulsive masturbator who had, when drunk, exposed himself twenty years before and never recovered from the guilt. This was in Newark. There was Eddie and the seventy hits of acid.

And more, more.

But J.D. was from Lane's decade. She knew West of Network, all the way through. They had sung it one night over a game of cards—and that was the fourth thing about the Motel: games of chance were every-where. She was blond and she had drunk too much in the state school and after, and she got her nickname—her real name was Jeannie Dolance—just because she had caused so much trouble when younger. After her aphasia set in though, her troub-lemaking was over. After that, she left her husband at home and moved in with her parents.

J.D. was on Eye Contact because of her wrists. Eye Contact meant you couldn't go anywhere but the Three North Lounge, and even then you had to have an orderly trailing you. All day. J.D. wasn't going any-where, anyway. The orderly just sat in the doorway, recording observations every five minutes. One time, Lane had caught a glimpse of one of these pads, where they scrawled these observations—a whole page cov-ered with the words "sleeping and breathing."

5) They had things like Status Three, which was

official recognition of the fact that you could leave the floor (the third floor north, where Lane and J.D. lived) to go to the soda machine, or to stare out the windows in the lobby. Status three was why Lane was allowed to go out to the steakhouse.

6) Television had therapeutic value, too, because in the Motel, except for the hour of group therapy in the morning, it was never off. Elena loved game shows. Game shows, and minor league baseball.

Valdez, the orderly with the gold front tooth, was covering J.D. that night, and between taking notes, she was flipping through an auto magazine. From where he stood, out in the hall, Lane could make out J.D.'s figure facing away, heaving with grief. She was definitely breathing.

He suppered on the Motel airplane food and went to the meeting upstairs, with the junkies on Three South, before coming back, and then he passed back and forth in the hall, on specious pretexts, unable to enter. Why not? What kind of fear keeps you from your friends when they are hurt? Later, though, amid the squabbling over evening medication, as he stood in line for the drugs they were using on him, he made up his mind. After he swallowed the pills, he knocked on her open door.

A single hand, braceleted in white gauze, waved him forward. He sat on the edge of her bed and curled himself over her. It was a moment when the Motel regulation (#7 the rule against physical contact) was forgiven. Valdez said nothing. J.D.'s eyes were tiny red slashes.

Lane told her that she looked great, and she tried to laugh. It looked like it hurt.

They were silent for a long time. Five or ten minutes.

Lane was thinking about his own past, which had come back to trouble him in those weeks. Shadows played on the wall in J.D.'s room, while he thought back, emblems of activity out in the hall. The residents passed down and back, from the lounge to the dining room and back again.

"Not like I'm a professional in the field or anything," Lane said, "but if you want to talk, talk. It could be good."

J.D. shook her head.

"I could tell you things," he said. "I could tell you about the weather outside. And downtown Short Hills."

He stood at the window. Outside J.D.'s room, the sun was just setting and its colors were like an act of arson. All of them in the Motel had missed spring this year, really, and it would take a whole year to get it back. Inside, it was sixty-eight year round. No seasons in the Motel.

"Trouble sleeping still?" he said.

J.D. rolled slowly away from him. The sheets clung to her.

There was another long silence, but then J.D. started to talk, and Lane knew she would. In the end, people gave it a try in the Motel. Because it was the end. Everyone took the place on its own terms, even if they held out for a while. So she started talking finally, confessing all sorts of things. She convicted herself of crimes in places she'd never visited.

The first important fact, she told him, was that she was a liar. She reached deep into her resources to confess, to tell Lane the truth—about how she couldn't be trusted: "I'll lie my way out of every situation. I lied about my detox to make everyone feel sorry for me. I lied to get tranquilizers for my detox. I lied to my mother and father about where I was going for the month. I lied to the admitting doctor."

Lane told her to go on. He had lied to the admitting doctor too.

"I lied about graduating college, I said I made it in four years. I lied about how much I drank. I exaggerated it. I lied about learning to swim, and being a virgin, all of that."

The ninth rule about the Motel was that everyone smoked, even the people who didn't smoke. The drugs were all gone, and the coffee was some chemical substitute, so cigarettes were the only meager route to destruction left. So Lane had taken up smoking, and now, in J.D.'s room, he was lighting up, because it was an emergency and Valdez, who was involved with the auto magazine, wasn't going to pay any attention. At the window, he watched the trees sway. The moon was coming up, and it was nearly full.

"These aren't big things," Lane said. "It's like anyone could do this stuff."

He knew she would just have to talk until she exhausted herself, so he just let her go on. After a while, J.D. developed a theme. She had violated every one of the Ten Commandments. That was her theme. And she wanted to tell him about it.

"Compare and contrast," Lane said. "We'll match them up."

He offered her a drag from the cigarette. Again he sat on the edge of the bed. The ashes tumbled upon the floor.

"I can't remember them so well," Lane said. "You remind me, okay?"

*　*　*

The stories there were all great, but they didn't follow really. The characters changed sexes. Space and time were violated. The second day in, when Lane woke after hours of semiconscious tossing with a case of the shakes, he'd taken a current events class with the two psychotics on the ward. This was a Status One thing you had to do. One of the others was a girl, Myra, no more than eighteen or nineteen, from the Jersey Shore, and the social worker who ran the class was trying to get her to read a single newspaper headline. A single headline. And she couldn't do it. She got about halfway—MOB BOSS, Lane remembered—and that was it. Meanwhile, he was having a conversation with the social worker about pollution, about the weird stuff washing up on the beaches. Even the older schizophrenic guy came out of a deep anti-psychotic nod to read a comic strip. But the girl couldn't do it. MOB BOSS BEATS RAP.

Later, Lane talked with her for a whole lunch about *Positive Outlook*, a book she was reading, that her family had given her. She couldn't summarize much there either. She probably couldn't read it at all. And she couldn't tell how sad it was that they'd given her that book—that meager assemblage of pulp and glue and print—to hold off what she was up against. Her wrists were crosshatched, up and down their lengths. She couldn't complete a coherent sentence. *Positive Outlook* was going to help? Myra got transferred to the state hospital, when her insurance ran out. And that was the last he knew of her.

These stories were full of gear changes. No surprise then that J.D.'s version of the first commandment had to do with how she went to this miracle cure place in the southern part of the state—a church where there was a minister who helped people to put down their crutches and take off their eye patches. It was hard to tell whether it really happened or not. Things were getting worse. She hadn't slept with her husband in a long, long time, and she had quit the job at the school, and she was lying around with the shades drawn. She was wishing hard for calamity. Then a girlfriend told her about this church. She went a few times. Then, at last, she spoke with the preacher.

He had a lot of advice about her condition. And the next time she went he called her up front to take the cure. In front of everybody. He told them about her. Rather than feel relieved, though, she just got panicky about the cure.

And it didn't work of course. She was standing up in her pew, in front of all these people. A moment of silence passed. She waited. That should have been it right there. Gladness ought to have surged through her. The most ancient thing, divine intervention, and the most modern, radiation, you couldn't be sure with either one. The organ started again, and the guy on her left, with the two canes, flung down his burdens and strode up the aisle to be blessed in person. There was a spring in his step.

And J.D. had smiled. She smiled like she had never smiled before. And she said, Boy, I feel better. She smiled her first smile in weeks and told the preacher she owed it all to him. Then she got out of there.

"Taking the Lord's name in vain," J.D. told Lane. "That's the first one. It's the first or second, anyway."

Lane nodded.

"See? I'm stuck with that for good. That's not going to just go away."

Lane stared down into the empty trash barrel, by her bedside table. He dropped the vestigial ember of his cigarette down into it. The shards of J.D.'s ashtray must have been in there, but it was empty now. They had emptied everything during the room search.

"Where's the crime?" he said. "That you went to this faith healer guy? Or that you went and claimed to be healed and went home feeling—"

"You don't get it," J.D. said, and she was right. "The point is that I wasn't cured because I'm not worth curing."

He thought about it. He went into her bathroom and unrolled a streamer of toilet paper. He carried it back to J.D. She took the tissue. She looked away.

"And there's this light that comes into my room at night, when I'm trying to sleep. It's like a light on the ceiling, or like a bunch of lights, or a map of the stars or something."

"They leave the lights on—"

"I'll put my hands over my eyes and the lights are still showing up on my hands. If I close my eyes the lights are still there, too. It's not a fucking ceiling light. I hid in the closet. But I couldn't sleep. Only daytime is bearable. Never sleeping—that's the only thing I can do to avoid it."

Lane nodded.

"Taking the Lord's name in vain," she said, "or graven image or whatever."

"Well, you'll sleep tonight," Lane said. "Don't worry about that."

He sat on the edge of her bed then, and as Valdez watched he brushed away the blond bangs from her forehead. And he didn't regret how they were all drugged in the Motel, how the guy who raved about Soviet interference in telecommunications stumbled like a sleepwalker when they gave him the halidol.

That's the thing people missed, how humane it could be. J.D. wouldn't see any lights for days, when they brought in those pills later.

So the Motel had its own logic, its logic of illness. It differed from induction or deduction, but in its own way it was just as exhaustive. That guy Anton who was arrested exposing himself he had never gotten over exposing himself, even though he had done it when he was drinking. Now he was very secretive. Even in language now, he worried about exposing too much. Meanwhile, whenever he was late for any therapy, or for volleyball or whatever, he was in his room jerking off.

And with Lane a lot of it had to do with dads. That was the thing. By the time he had moved back in with his mom, he found dads wherever he looked, in lines at the supermarket, examining goods at mall department stores, each with their advice about hardware and job advancement, each with a word of encouragement or support.

Now that his past had surfaced, like some barnacled submarine, he spent his days thinking of his own father's empty eyes, and all the stories lost inside his father's skull, bits of Lane that had vanished never to be gathered up again. Memories like lighthouse beacons flickering in a heavy storm. Since then he knew himself to be partial, unwhole, unfinished, not fully born. But that was what it was like in the Motel, and the fifteen different kinds of therapy—drugs, behaviorism, cognitive therapy, group therapy, drama therapy, art therapy, individual treatment—these were just a different logic, one meant to halt your downward spiral through bombardment so you could see it for what it was, a weak force, a statistical error.

* * *

"Well, what about the rest of them?" Lane asked her.

"The commandments?"

He nodded.

"There's the big A."

She balled the drenched tissue and hurled it toward the plastic trashcan.

"Three times I committed adultery."

Lane feigned concern.

"Did you tell him?" he said. "Sometimes you know—"

"It wasn't against my husband. I wouldn't do that. It was before that. It was with the boyfriend before my husband."

"Wait," Lane said.

"It's the spirit of it," J.D. said. She was shivering, and she wound the bedclothes around herself like some gigantic bandage. "And my spirit is all dead. I'm dead inside."

"Hmm," Lane said. "So you're trying to think your way out of it?"

Her closet door was open, and Lane stood in front of it, waiting out a long silence. A clump of laundry was mashed down on the floor—drab lingerie, a half dozen variations on the same blank sweatshirt—where J.D. must have spent the night, hiding from the phantom lights she had generated.

"And I didn't speak to my parents. I didn't honor them. Second generation immigrants. But so what? Me, me, always me."

"Oh, come on," Lane said. He shut the closet door. "Sometimes maybe you honor your parents by leaving them alone. I don't know. It's not like I—"

"And I stole a lot. Everyone I knew was stealing. And I took stuff that wasn't useful. Totally useless. It was just to steal. I took a tape measurer or spaghetti tongs or something."

"Forget about it, J.D." He paced now, and something in the room was different. It was late. Valdez had disappeared from her post. "I mean, I stole drugs from this dealer guy in my high school. I stole what was already illegal, and then I sold it back to him. I persuaded him that it wasn't me, and then a little later, I persuaded him to buy back his own stuff. This was nothing. No big deal. What about yourself? How about the way you maybe fucked yourself up?"

He stood at the foot of her bed. He lit another cigarette.

"Didn't keep Sundays holy? Big deal. You could have used a day off, right?"

He hadn't raised his voice, but a sort of a conviction formed in Lane, and it was a novel feeling, to have conviction. It was right and good, Lane thought—and he thought those very words, *right and good*—that Thou Shalt Not Kill Thyself. And he wanted to let J.D. in on this, even if he didn't even know where to start.

At ten-thirty the residents of the Motel proceeded in an unruly column to their rooms, where each and every one of them faced up to the fact that they were afraid of the dark. Lane, preoccupied with his own dignity even after three weeks, usually tried to turn in before his roommate—a former dealer of cocaine from Shipbottom, N.J. Lane tried to fall asleep over a book, so that it would appear involuntary, so that the dealer wouldn't know. But on the first of the month, he was still in J.D.'s room, when Valdez came in, pointing to her watch. Lane was sitting on the edge of the bed, holding J.D.'s wrist, as though the gauze there were the finest jewelry, holding her bandaged hand with his fractured one.

"I know," he said to the orderly.

"Well, get a move on then," Valdez said.

Valdez brought more pills for J.D. Lane listened for the deceleration of her breathing, after she swallowed them. He just waited, listening. Reflex or no reflex, breathing predated the most ancient of writings; it was older than the oldest civilization. There were theories of transit from wrong breathing to right, but no rules.

J.D. reached for the lamp next to her bed. Only the light from the corridor splashed weakly over them. "Promise me you'll stay alive through tomorrow night," he said.

J.D. didn't promise.

Valdez came back in and threw the switch on the ceiling light. It was like being caught in the backseat of the car on prom night. "Out," she said.

Lane stood.

"Sleep well," Lane said.

"I'll try."

Out in the corridor, Linda waited for him. They walked down the corridor together. Linda was smiling.

"You understand, you should tell me what the two of you discussed. It's for her sake."

They stood in front of the door to his room. In the awkward silence, forgetting all he had learned in the Motel about the importance of making eye contact, Lane looked at his slippered feet and listened to the metronomic snoring of his roommate. Out like a light. He said, "Answer a question first?"

Linda nodded.

"How do I know when I'm cured?"

Alice finally moved out on the first of May and the first thing she did was try to get Dennis to take her in. She tried to leave home and move in down the street, into the Francis' place, or at least she asked Dennis, who was talking to her again, though it wasn't exactly cordial. His mom happened also to be Lane's mom, though, and it just wasn't going to fly. She hadn't expected much. So she moved in with Scarlett, who was leaving soon anyway to go back to Ohio. Alice could assume her lease in the apartment over the exterminator's place, and that would be that.

There was no big scene when she moved her stuff —her mother was out for the afternoon. Alice left by mass transit, with her guitars and a single duffle bag, making only one trip back for her practice amp. The rest of the stuff she threw in a packing box in the middle of her room. She just left it there. Alice moved by herself.

On the way out, she opened the shades in her room. She opened the windows. It seemed like years since she had last seen bright daylight. That evening the light was clear and hope seemed almost unavoidable. When the room was empty, she caught the bus. From the bus stop, in the center of town, she rolled the amp on its casters to the exterminator's place.

"Not gonna play that inside I hope," he said from his post.

She buzzed up. A minute passed. She eyed the exterminator. He watched the traffic. Things in Haledon slowed because of the warmer weather. Finally, Scarlett's keys fell out of the sky.

When she got halfway up the second flight she cursed. She screamed Scarlett's name. Used to be she spent most of her time moving equipment. It was only a month and a half since she moved the amp home.

Scarlett grabbed the casters at the bottom of the front end and they came off in her hand. The two of them teetered on the stairs for a moment—and Alice imagined a wrist fracture or other breakage—but they managed to regain control, to get the amplifier up into Scarlett's apartment: this amp that might never see a wall socket again.

Scarlett got out of the way as Alice dragged her burden in and settled it in the middle of the room. "Listen"—she told Alice—"Dennis called."

Alice asked what he wanted. "Do you have anything to drink? It's fucking hot."

Scarlett reached for glasses. The drinks were in the blender.

"No idea."

Dennis' attitude was bad since Lane had disappeared. She had told Scarlett before but she just wanted to tell it again.

"Do you think I should call him?"

"I don't know," Scarlett said. She served the highballs. She set them on the coffee table. On plastic coasters. "What do you think?"

"I was kinda settled on never talking to him again."

"Well, but you were—" Scarlett said.

"That's different," Alice said.

"So don't call then."

"So I won't."

They settled down in front of the television and drank and watched the evening game show stuff. Every now and then Alice mumbled a correct answer (careful always to phrase it in a question, according to the rules of the program), but otherwise it was quiet.

Scarlett worked days, now, as a waitress in a coffee shop. It was a step up from the health food place, but she hadn't adjusted to the hours yet. After the network movie came and went neither of them could stay awake. They went to bed without eating. Alice slept on the couch, and Scarlett slept in the bed.

When she woke, Alice had the place to herself. She made coffee, and the smell of it—Krakatoa brand— filled the apartment. She watched some Metalheads on a talk show. Metalheads and their parents.

No days were as provisional as these.

Then the phone rang again.

Since the answering machine was broken—it made a tangle of loops and knots out of cassettes—Alice decided to answer the phone herself. She weakened. She actually ran to catch it. She ran, thinking on the way there, that it was too stupid. It couldn't be Dennis. It was.

"I'm making coffee," Alice said. And she carried the phone—it had an immense cord the length of which, even in its snarled condition, could travel to any corner of the apartment—to the old, scorched percolator.

He told her he had called before. She told him she had been unpacking things. He told her he had called twice, and then Dennis told her he would keep it short, that he didn't want to get involved anymore. But he didn't want to not talk. Everywhere people were having those feuds; at every gathering you could count on two people refusing to speak who used to be close. Silence prevailed. Somebody had to put his foot down. Dennis wanted to apologize. He had wanted things to go differently. And then Dennis told her that Max was going to call. Max had this idea.

"Why didn't Max call himself?"

"I dunno," Dennis said, "you know him. I volunteered."

"What's your fucking problem, anyway?" Alice said. "I don't get the whole thing. What you guys are—"

Dennis interrupted. He was back to that tone that he had at L.G.'s party, up on the roof—a crisis-management tone. "I'm trying to do you a favor, and you don't even know what it is. Max just wants to straighten things out too."

"Forget it," Alice said. "Forget it. I don't want to straighten anything. People keep bringing up shit from years ago."

"Like what? You don't even—"

"Yeah, if you're so fucking concerned why didn't you let me—"

"I'm moving out. I'm working a lot of extra jobs," he said. "I'm staying out of there. And anyway my stepmother—"

"Listen, I don't give a fuck," Alice said.

"I'm just letting you know in case you want to. Max, I mean."

"Forget it, all right?"

She holstered the phone in its sheath and plunged onto the couch. It was a few minutes, staring blankly into Scarlett's blank apartment, before the scrawled note on the coffee table caught her eye. Scarlett's script was a florid dainty affair, precise in its abberations and enlargements. The note was titled and underlined at the top. GUIDELINES FOR MY APARTMENT. Subhead: A COUPLE OF REMINDERS.

Evelyn Smail and Ruthie Francis sat stiffly in Ruthie's living room as Ruthie confessed the whole story to her, her new version of how he had evaporated before her eyes where he had been so promising, the new story about how, frankly, she had known all along it would happen. She might have been a reader of evidence, might have seen it, and read its cryptograms. It was a failure that would take a while to expiate. She cried noiselessly, daintily, in subtle unassuming rivulets. She directed blame, without choking up, at Lane's father. Maybe Lane's blankness—because that was the right name for it now—was an homage to his father, who had himself slipped through all gradations of self to be all but entirely gone. Lane's unavoidable love of his father. You could take the father out of the town, Ruthie theorized, but not the dad out of the son.

In the midst of the next silence, they sipped an herb tea which calmed as advertised, or at least coincided with the inactivity of the moment, and which tasted like extra-strength cleaning agents or turpentine. Evelyn had called Ruthie's husband to ask if he needed a ride home from the station. She had cooked for Ruthie, canceled her appointments.

Evelyn believed she had no real gift for conversation, at least not like Ruthie's gift, Ruthie's ability to move restlessly through crowds and sow concord. But now she saw how it was not always the most pleasant skill. In silence in the living room, Evelyn lost herself in thoughts of the past. Where there was conversation she listened to it all and found she was a good listener, that listening was easy. She remembered how it had worked so well with troubled teens, with seniors, with the children at the day care center.

"The visiting rooms are so severe, and there are outbursts from the others," Ruthie said suddenly. "It's exactly like you heard, the details are just what you've heard, but the effect is so different. And this was just in the lobby, the main floor. On Sunday I go back."

Evelyn asked where they ate.

"There's some kind of point system for good behavior—so they let him go across the street. He was surprised about the heat. He was talking about all kinds of things. He was talking about times he had shoplifted ten years ago. On a field trip to Niagara Falls in his eighth grade year, he stole a simulated piece of uranium from a hydroelectric plant tour or something. This was the kind of thing on his mind. He doesn't look better to me. He looks like he hasn't slept in weeks. He's white as a sheet."

"Well, but it's a long way—" Evelyn said.

On in this way. Waiting for Foster, her husband, to land at the station in Paterson.

Ruthie seemed to have forgotten all about Dennis. Or maybe it was Dennis himself who had forgotten about her. Perhaps in this juncture of sunspots and orbits the opportunity to leave had come to him. And Evelyn wondered what would do it for Alice. What had it done for her, Evelyn, in the past? What was the calculus that finally enabled youth to pass, for good, out of youth? This generation never seemed to leave home. They grew up to a certain point and then spent the next decade, until collapse, trying to recapture the novelty of adolescence, that pulse of youth that seems, in its fullest bloom, permanent.

A feather duster lay on the mantle above Evelyn, and she thought about taking it up. Dust was settling in Ruthie's house.

"Alice will be leaving soon, too," she said.

They sipped their tea.

"How do you feel about it?" Ruthie asked.

"I guess I must be bluffing," she said.

Gentility hung on. Sunlight streamed across the dusty surfaces. A beautiful afternoon, an afternoon that smiled on the suburbs. Evelyn gathered up the tea service—china rattled on silver—and headed for the kitchen. The mysterious simplicity of boiling water, the primeval chemistry of tea steeping. She would make more.

Friday p.m. Max driving feeling bad, bad about himself, about things, driving block after block all leveled in Paterson all totally flattened, bricked-over windows, boarded over windows, homes no longer homes, guys with concealed weapons hanging out on corners, guys with unconcealed weapons. D.U.I. Max cruised by the Krakatoa coffee factory where Nails was no longer employed. The days of spring all stretched out in his mind.

On his way to DD's Paterson lunch establishment, overlooking the white waters of the Passaic, but weaving along the roads windows rolled down radio up loud. What was that? A lamppost, guy in front of a lamppost. Somebody going to pick up. A car horn. The Doppler effect. Max was feeling fine. Either gotta stop working so much or face the exhaustion. Stop working was probably the right choice.

Lane stuck in Short Hills, too, that was the funniest thing, same fucking hospital. His brother was in the same hospital. Fucking unbelievable hospital, gymnasium and painting studio. The food was okay. Sound mind, sound body. No radios though, not allowed to have radios, but classical music, fucking violin players some weekends to entertain them. Different ward though Lane was on the drink and despair ward, double threat, and his kid brother downstairs with the juveniles. Poor fucking Tony Crick, eighteen years old.

He pulled his car into the parking lot. Empty everywhere. Whole fucking state was empty. They all head out to the shore first big weekend in May, all get a jump on the national holiday. Bodily parts washing up on the shore. He was stuck in town and he was D.U.I. but he would no longer fret. Diminished capability brought with it diminished idea of causality: he was not surprised, as he parked his borrowed car in front of the lot by DD's, about the two of them in the hospital, or about Alice Smail waiting for him there.

They didn't discuss it. They just walked in. Max went first. Low-visibility, high decibels, the regular clientele. Neither said too much at the outset, neither was surprised to be there. DD's was a bar. Alice and he had things *not* to talk about, so they just didn't for a while.

But he asked her what she drank and she drank bourbon so they both drank bourbon. Maybe Alice was the only girl with dyed blonde hair and black fingernail polish in DD's, but she looked great. She was starting to look like she belonged there. Her style was dwindling or becoming popular, one of the two. The other guys in there were even checking her out, Max thought. Couple of years ago they might have looked sideways at her, but they were thinking Alice was pretty darned cute now. Max worked up to what he wanted to say—well he tried to work up to it—but then he never ended up saying it. Alice interrupted the silence. She asked why he asked Dennis to call. Max said Dennis had volunteered.

Then they said nothing for a while.

"I don't know," he said, finally, desperately. "How do I know? Thing is though, maybe I wanted to make it up to you. You know, about what happened. I mean, it was Lane and not us, but I wanted to make it up to you. Because—"

Alice waited.

"And maybe if, I mean, if we wanted to, we could apologize to him, because I think I know how to get to him, see. Because of my brother being in there. In the same hospital. So I know how to get to him, and maybe I just wanted to tell you, because you know I wasn't trying to fuck him up or anything—"

Alice didn't say anything.

They sipped the drinks.

"Your brother?" she said.

"Yeah, he's getting out soon, though. It's meant to be like a short term place. They're gonna maybe transfer him to the state place in Trenton. He'll be out real soon."

"Does he still—"

"You mean with the—"

"He's—" Alice said.

"He's a real mess," Max said. "Stuff with dresses: that's just the tip of the iceberg."

"Well, but what's the deal anyway?" Alice said.

Max thought. The jukebox in DD's was playing—

"Because they keep your mail there and they monitor your visitors and your phone calls and everything. You can, like, keep whoever you want from visiting you and you won't get their mail or anything. But the thing is I could get a message to him. Or like my brother could get a message to him if that's what you want. We could get him to—"

Mike, at the bar, refilled the drinks. Max was trying not to slur. He had speech therapy enunciation.

"That is, if you want."

"What the fuck is in it for you?"

"Oh shit I dunno," Max said. "Don't ask me stuff like that."

"Well, listen," Alice said. "I got a lot on my mind now 'cause of moving out of my mother's place and trying to get a job and thinking maybe of going back to school—I'm gonna be like in the record business or maybe open a used clothing store or something— and one thing I'm not doing is thinking about this shit. Like all of this is his problem really. And I sorta liked the guy, but big fucking deal if I never see him again or anything. I got plans. Know what I mean? So I appreciate the offer—even though I think it's a little crass—and I think you're okay, Max, but enough already, right?"

That was the end of that. They stayed for two or three more selections on the jukebox, the usual racket, for a couple more drinks. There was compensation in this world: Max would just drink fast, drink in silence, drink—whenever he could—in solitude.

The place was packed solid now with the first evening rush. Except for the jukebox there was almost no conversation. Mike, at the bar, was talking to himself. Everyone in there was whispering bitterly to himself.

"Are you gonna be able to drive?" Alice asked.

"Sure, sure," Max said. "Don't even—"

"I'll take you," she said. "I'll go back with you."

"Write a letter," Max was trying to say, "write a letter and tell him what you said, that you like him and stuff, and I'll have the kid deliver it. That's the way—"

"I could call a cab or something. It's better than waiting for the bus."

"A bus?" Max said, as though his voice would not carry. "This is fucking New Jersey."

The door was swinging closed behind them. Evening again. The season's first swarm of mosquitos hovered densely around them. Alice called from the wall phone by the hardware store. When the cab came, Max slumped over in the seat. Alice piled in after him.

He asked her to come home with him, but she couldn't understand the words now. She didn't answer. As they drove up the hill into Haledon, and then up the cliff into the heights, to the trailer where Max lived, she held his sleeping head on her shoulder. It was a sort of necrophilia, but it was okay. She hauled Max into the trailer, when they got there, and spread him out on the floor. He was mumbling and protesting. But even when he grabbed her tights, she didn't pay any attention. She left the lights on, the tape deck playing swamp music, and then she took off. No one would take advantage of Max Crick where he lay. No one could take more advantage of him than he had himself.

Dennis was running again. Three weeks he had been running now, and he was running again and there was nothing athletic about it. Shin splints crippled him. His muscles knotted and cramped, his mouth was always dry. His body was ten years older than the rest of him. He was not his natural age. But he was out, running along the railroad tracks. He knew he ran all wrong, like some web-footed thing, as though he had spent years horseback riding. But he ran. And today he got this idea of catching a ride on the freight train when it passed. The tradition of running, the tradition of the messenger hurrying to his own execution, it was growing on him. And what he figured he would do here, was just take advantage of the freight trains of Haledon and get out of town for the night. Into Paterson, or maybe up into the woods. Wherever it went.

Friday night. No big deal. The radical, tactical conclusion to which Dennis had come in these weeks, in these days of jogging three-quarters of a mile, and then a mile, and then back down to three-quarters, and finally up to a mile-and-a-quarter, through showers, fitful sunshine, heavy winds, through moments of gravity and of levity, his limbs protruding from unfashionable athletic gear like the limbs of unfed poultry, was that what he really wanted to do now, whatever the fuck was happening at home, or happening to like housing starts or durable goods or something, whatever was happening, what he really wanted was to ask Scarlett on a date. He had known it since that night he put her to bed, that Saturday night. As he ran, now, he grabbed for the ladder on the back side of this refrigeration car, but he couldn't get hold of it.

Because her blond spikes were the greatest, and because beneath the baggy dresses she wore were round, maternal hips and because she let people talk and didn't cut them off or anything. She didn't get panicked in a crisis. She smiled sympathetically at complete strangers. There was him and her left and it just seemed like a good idea.

Dennis leapt for the handle by the couplings on the side of a chlorine tank car—it was shaped like an aspirin substitute *caplette* or like a nuclear sub—and he got ahold of it this time. He climbed aboard. And since it was not an electric train—because there were no high tension lines there, no pyrotechnical sparks—he climbed right up on top. He thought about highway overpasses. New Jersey was the world's longest running silent comedy. Standing straight up as the train started down the hill now, Dennis was the owner of all he saw, circling back around forever. It wasn't a way out; it was just a way to see the sights.

6 / The Pinnacle, the coffee shop where Alice had worked when she was a kid, when she saved for electric guitars, it wasn't too far from Scarlett's, and late on Fridays it emptied out—she remembered— except for insomniac philosphers, victims of heart-break, lovers of jazz, and their kin. The short order cooks spent Friday nights attending to countertop spills and sharpening ancient blades. No one spoke, except to remark on how the pool halls of Haledon had once housed the most dangerous of night clubs. Retired drummers were debated and which was the saddest ballad ever sung.

But mostly the Pinnacle was a tomb. No vista was visible from its heights. It was miles downhill from any pinnacle. Still, towards midnight, Alice took the pad with Scarlett's regulations on it, made a ball of the top sheet—the faint indentations of Scarlett's pen-manship remained—and headed there anyway.

Alice was no writer. She didn't write letters like Scar-lett did—long, impeccable confessions sealed in colored envelopes—or even blunt, businesslike postcards like those she sometimes got from her dad. Anyway, the way Alice saw it, everything was against the harsh light of letters. Answering machines endangered letters. But after she left Max on the floor of his apartment, something in Alice gave. What Max had said was like a deathbed request. And the thing she realized, walking down Haledon Ave., smoking and thinking, was that if it was a last chance situation she would try to put things right with Lane. She would have put things right with Mike Maas, for example. She wouldn't have told his girlfriend, Suzy Drummond, to go ahead and sleep with that other guy, if she knew Mike was gonna set himself on fire.

Or maybe it was just she knew she was going to spend a lot of nights alone after Scarlett moved back west, and she didn't want to spend them in Dover's trying to get some kid to remove her tights. She just wanted to set things right before getting older. It was that time.

And that was why she decided to write to Lane and maybe to say something about April Fool's.

The letter started to bug her as soon as she got herself into the Pinnacle, though. An admirable decision doesn't necessarily add up to a great letter. She sat at the counter and watched the demoralized counter guy fill endless cups of coffee up and down the aisle. The blank sheet lay in front of her. She scribbled in the margins.

When he ambled back her way, foul rag clutched in one hand, Alice asked if they had decaffeinated coffee. The waiter pointed to a huge vat of mix. Krakatoa.

"All we got."

"Perfect," Alice said, and then, "and, hey, I got a question for you. I got something I want to ask you. Nothing personal, but you mind if I ask how long you worked here?"

His back was turned. He shrugged.

He spooned the mix into a stained mug, and the action was slow and precise. In the absence of some regular coffee shop hustle he was making the most of every opportunity.

Nothing had changed in the Pinnacle since she worked there. The stools, upholstered in a red vinyl were still patched with black electrical tape. The marsh scenes that adorned the walls, lacquered with some plastic finish, were marred with the same splotches of grease and soda and mustard which stained them long ago. Here and there a pat of butter still fouled the off-white tiles on the ceiling.

"Been here six months." He set the cup and saucer down on the counter in front of her. He was Mediterranean, Alice figured, with a dark complexion and exaggerated features—brow and nose and ears—as though he'd been dipping into steroids. He could have been a weightlifter or track and field guy.

She wondered if they paid him less than minimum wage. If he was connected with organized crime. If he had a visa or a green card, or whatever other bureaucratic stuff he needed to be on the Jersey work force.

"Where do you come from?" She said it kind of loud. She wasn't thinking so much about what it would sound like, as usual, and the guys at the end of the counter fell silent and looked her way. "I mean you come from Italy or something right?"

He rang up a check, spindling it with a real flourish.

He counted back the change under his breath. Five nighthawks remained in the Pinnacle. The place was lit up like a Christmas tree.

Where Alice might have let the guy go, figuring that he wasn't going to answer, that he didn't want to, that he didn't talk to a girl in fishnet stockings after midnight in Haledon, N.J., but she just didn't want to. It was proof of the fact that you could have a change of heart about one small thing and still have deep pockets of poor behavior remaining in your personality.

"'Cause what I'm curious about," she went on, when he passed nearby to mop off the front of the milk machines, "is writing home. How you go about it and stuff. Because—"

She finished the decaffeinated sludge and pointed to her cup again.

"'Cause I'm trying to write to someone is all and I don't know how to start or anything. I haven't seen them and I want to start it and I don't know."

He took her cup away, rinsed it quickly and went back to the vat of mix.

There was a guy in the back room who came out now. The new manager, maybe, or the new owner. The two of them had a spirited exchange in a language that seemed to have only vowels. They looked her way and they laughed, just a chuckle. And then they returned to their regimental cleaning. First this machine and then that. The manager guy began to stack some of the chairs at the booths—upside down on the tables.

It was just a chuckle but Alice didn't take it well. Suddenly, she felt really bad, really irredeemably bad, worse than she had in weeks. She had sunk to where she was one of those people who found companionship only after midnight in conversations with non-English-speaking counterpersons in coffee shops. She couldn't even get down a little bit of contrition on paper.

Human bonds all broke up, fragmented, shattered, *exploded*, she thought right then, resolution or no resolution, according to whatever explosives were at hand, and that was what she really wanted to tell Lane, but she didn't see that it had much to do with him, especially because it was she, Alice, who was a breaker of bonds, a violator of families, a dead soul on the eternal Garden State Thruway of dead souls. Just seeing the two Italian or Greek or Turkish guys, whatever they were, two guys with a *homeland*, stacking chairs and telling jokes in their language about *pussy* or something, it made everything worse. Only the immigrants in America seemed to have homes. Only they knew how to speak of the past.

"Hey, listen," she said, sliding off the stool, and heading over to where they were standing. "I worked here before, right, and the thing is now I've just moved out of my mom's house and I'm a little down on like my luck or something, whatever, and the thing is I really need a job. I have to get a job. I have to get some money together. I can only live for like two or three more weeks on the money I have—I can only pay for this place I'm living for that long—and I'm wondering if maybe you guys need some help, because I worked here before is what I'm saying and maybe like could I fill out an application?"

The waiter looked at the manager/owner guy and smiled and said *application*. And the other guy shook his head.

"Says no application," the waiter said. "Says no opening."

"But let me just—"

"No opening," the waiter said.

"Fill one out," Alice said.

Both men shook their heads.

"Oh fuck," Alice said.

And she walked back to the stool, to the pad there, and she whispered to herself—and scrawled it right afterwards, right in the midst of those scribbled circles and triangles and bits of forlorn geometry—"Oh well, I fucked everything up and I'm really sorry about it. I never thought that maybe the best thing is just to leave people alone sometimes. I never thought I was hurting you just because I was lonely. So that's that and maybe I'll see you when you get out."

The waiter spindled her check with the same verve as he had the last, and he directed her attention, while ringing up the register, to a bowl of encrusted candies—small white pillowshaped things with garish bits of jelly oozing from them, some sort of fiendish medicine, some last reward. Alice took a handfull and headed for the payphone in the doorway.

Max's answering machine squeaked so much you couldn't make out the message but it was some kind of Christian metal thing, the Lord saith let him that heareth me heedeth me, blah, blah, blah, and Alice said "You're probably still passed out, and I don't think any of this is gonna work, but I mean even if I'm taking care that I'm like doing the honorable thing or whatever, right? So maybe it's better just to wait. Maybe doing nothing is doing the right thing. Drink a lot of fruit juice when you wake up."

The Garden State had more malls than any state in these territories. The first mall ever was in the Garden State (as was the first Blimpies), near Paramus, and they broke ground for it almost fifty years ago, in a moment of great public and political consensus about the coming of malls. Its gigantic fallout shelter underneath would protect those lucky enough to be shopping at the time of Bergen County's nuclear destruction. A wealth of goods and services would remain for these lucky shoppers.

Though the interior of the Paramus Park Mall had been modernized since that time, the structure itself was still a homely public space. It looked like a reform school or psychiatric hospital when compared with the malls of the Jersey shore, with those stylish docks and piers.

But that was New Jersey innovation. This was the state where professional baseball was first played (in Jersey City), where the first trade union was organized (in Haledon, of silk factory workers from Paterson), where Aaron Burr had his duel (in Weehawken). It was the state with the most traveled pavement in America. An historical place. The state that first sold malted milkshakes and filtered cigarettes. Lapels were narrow then. Parking spaces were wider. Shopping bags were made of paper. Bergen County was the seat of much change. So when Louis Giolas had completed his job interview with the gigantic carpet outlet at the Paramus Park Mall, where, in a bid for personal advancement, he was hoping to become one of the store managers, he thought he'd take a spin around like he used to when he was a kid.

L.G. had spruced up all right. He'd shined his tassled loafers. He'd borrowed cufflinks from his father. His hair was neatly parted and blown dry. He wore pleated trousers, a permanent press shirt with a button-down collar. A tie clip. He'd come a long way. Some days it seemed like he had. L.G. had been anxious about his interview. He'd arrived thirty minutes early.

After the L.T.D. Carpet Company, L.G. went through ValueRite, a feature of all malls in the area. VALUERITE—MADE FAMOUS IN AMERICA. He was drawn in by the power tools, though ValueRite was now better known for its cut-rate home loans and retail brokerage.

The interview, about which he was brooding as he walked, hefting picks and scythes, sledgehammers and pruning shears, ratchets and axes, had gone okay. He had promise, the way it seemed—

Past the men's department, he exited into the vast corridors of Paramus Park Mall. In the Grand Concourse, stands were lined up around the halfhearted fountains—sprinklers, really, L.G. thought—stands that sold the cheapest plastic stuff: watches with bootlegged, trademarked pictures on them, plastic earrings, holographs of naked thighs and breasts, plastic unicorns, plastic children holding hands. There was a booth that sold knives. In the grand concourse, a crowd had formed around a girl in black tights and a black lace brassiere who was lip-synching to precorded dance numbers. Everywhere in the throng, too, were black tights, black leather jackets, black rubber bangles.

L.G. was past the era of the girl singing in the mall, now, or maybe he had matters of employment on his mind: the interview had gone well, and the guy—with his balding pate, red nose, reddish swellings under his eyes—had a firm handshake. The guy shook L.G.'s hand like he knew quality. A life spent on a certain business, though it might be an unglamorous business like carpeting or power tools or sportswear or health and beauty aids, could have a certain dignity. What other conclusion could he come to now? What other choice could he make? The Garden State, in fact, was totally founded on guys like L.T.D. Carpet Company. He could see how it maybe didn't fit with this plan to be a rock and roll personality, but one day you just trusted what you had fallen into and went on from there.

Some of the other stores in the mall that L.G. passed: leather goods, shoestores, discount eyewear, greeting cards, three large chain department stores, an outlet store for one of the high-class mail-order catalogues —it was going out of business—several boarded up storefronts which boasted PARDON OUR APPEARANCE, as they probably had for years. And then in the most distant, untraveled corner of the mall there was a store which sold nothing but comic books, drug paraphernalia, and black light posters. When L.G. had thought enough about business for the morning, he went back there.

He remembered when he used to come to the comic book store, when he had ridden his bike ten miles from Haledon just to go there. The gangsters from downtown traveled that far, too, and they hung out in this empty dead-end of the mall and put cigarettes out in the planters, and breathed in the helium from helium balloons and, speaking in that dialect, they ranked on one another. He remembered when some older tough had cornered him. (Who was it with him? He had totally forgotten. Thinking back on it, it was maybe Mike Maas, before Mike had gotten all weird.) Anyway, these toughs had cornered him and Mike and asked if they smoked cigarettes. Well of course they did, but the guys said no, no you don't, you're fucking lightweights. And L.G. said, no way, he would prove it to them. He could inhale. More than that even, he could fucking inhale nasally. Out the mouth and into the nose, that French inhaling thing.

They did this, Mike and he did it, like performing monkeys for the toughs—these guys with acne and bad teeth, with dads who used belts on them and stuff—Mike and L.G. competing to inhale this dumb way, and the guys seemed like maybe they were gonna go for it after all, because they finally got around to talking about comic books, and the toughs favored the same titles as L.G. They goofed on each other, talked about drugs they had not yet done, women they had not yet loved. And then when Mike and L.G. went back out to the front of the mall where their bikes were parked, they didn't have any bikes at all. Somebody had hacksawed the chains they had used. The bikes were gone.

The toughs had set them up. The toughs were just killing time while a crime was being committed. The toughs vanished from the scene.

This was right by the comic book store. So L.G. was remembering the bench in the middle of the atrium right there, the potted palms, the little fountain, and on Saturday morning this very bench was occupied by Max Crick. Only L.G. didn't recognize that it was him at first. He thought maybe it was a street person or something. Max was slumped over, in one of those exaggerated postures of despair. His face was swollen and gray, his hair and clothes disordered and wild.

Max looked like he didn't have anywhere to go.

"Yo," L.G. trumpeted. He felt stupid in his clothes. In the duds.

"Hey."

And L.G. sat, and they were both sitting there thinking then, with as much room as they could get between them on the bench, the way guys will, guys being together.

L.G. told him how he was here for an interview—

it was the first thing out his mouth really—and that accounted for the duds, and when Max didn't ask he told him anyway that it was for a position at the L.T.D. Carpet Company. When Max didn't really offer anything on that either—and L.G. was a little relieved about it, because he didn't really want to get into it—he reminisced about Comix Comics and how it hadn't changed in this whole decade. The guy with the beard and the pony tail still ran it. He still smoked a pipe. They still played metal through the sound system.

When there was no way around it L.G. finally asked what he was doing up at the mall at 10:30 on a Saturday morning.

"Just came out," Max said, "you know, the majesty of it. I wanted to see the shoppers in all their glory and stuff."

L.G. nodded. He lit a cigarette and offered Max one, and he flicked the match into a planter by the bench. Old times.

"I just got fucking fired again. That's the thing," Max said, "I got the worst hangover, and I just couldn't get it together to, like, head down to the truck and stuff. And that was that. When I called in—"

"Shit, man," L.G. said.

"Like I wanted the fucking job in the first place," Max said.

"Jobs—" L.G. said.

"So I came down here," Max said, "to hole up in the movies for like three days."

Movies occupied the third floor of the mall. The octoplex movie palace.

"It's so fucking hot already," Max said, "it's only May and already it's fucking 85 fucking degrees and humid."

"Definitely," L.G. said. He didn't know where to start.

"Let's go see that girl sing, man. They got this girl singing, singing along with tapes in the middle of the mall. I saw her on the way in."

The usual crowd of dropouts was coming out of Comix Comics now. The usual aliens.

"How are you gonna play," Max said, "if you have to be carpet manager?"

"I'm gonna play," L.G. said, "I'm putting some stuff down on four tracks right now. But like I gotta butter my bread, you know? I mean, I can't even afford re-hearsal space in fucking Paterson, unless—"

Max didn't say anything.

"Let's go watch that girl sing—"

They rose and headed down the long open space, past families—bickering and sullen conglomerations of discomfort—bearing their loads of packages and bags, little kids dripping things on their chins, un-chaperoned pairs of teenagers. L.G. was worn out. It wasn't even eleven and he had gone from arguing that he was the right man for the job to regretting that he even wanted one.

"Hey Max," he said, "let's go get a drink. Can you get a drink in this place?"

"It's mall, man, it's a mall. Totally dry. Don't have anything in it but fast food and movies and artificial fabrics. Gotta get out into Paramus. Lotta bars in Paramus."

The crowd was dense around the singing girl now. Either she was a different one or she had changed into a bright yellow skin diving outfit. The sound was the same. She puckered her lips. They headed out amid the monotonous beat of the mall girl, out to the vast multi-tiered parking lot, that shadowy world of radio silence and impatient manuevering.

Inside L.G.'s mother's luxury sedan, they got the tape player going—it was a removable one that L.G. had hidden under the front seat—and eased out onto the Garden State Thruway. So what if the tape player ate tapes? So what if the average speed on the thruway was 15 m.p.h? So what if the past gave way to steadily diminishing expectations? Max pointed out the spot where Alice's mom's car had started by itself and hit the divider. There was still a skidmark there.

"Listen," Max said, "you know what we oughta do, we oughta go out to the car wash where Nails Pennebaker is working. We oughta go on out there and check him out. Not in any rush or anything, are you?"

They tried to pacify the residents. In the Motel, they had paint-by-number sets they used in art therapy. They rented videocassettes of G-rated comedies. And they had musical entertainments. It was reliable that the music they would choose for the entertainment would be enough to disturb anyone who was not already medicated. Some kind of deadly kiddy music. Sea chanties, or television theme songs. But everyone would be required to go, the head of the ward would strenuously suggest it, and most would agree to attend. When two or three of them refused—Eddie, for example—it would be pointed out that in fact it was not a suggestion but a requirement. The idea was to make you make the only logical decision. Lane did.

So they headed for the elevator Saturday afternoon, after they had the afternoon movie which you also couldn't avoid. There was a social worker who worked the videotape machine, and she was going to take them to the lobby area—a sort of glassed in garden area—to hear the *musicale*. Lane was surprised at how cute he thought the social worker was. She was maybe twelve years older than he was, and she wore bright lipstick and styled her red hair in this sloppy way that must have taken hours to perfect. It was the newest thing that came over him in the Motel. The first faint stirring of a libido.

Elena and Eddy and Anton and the rest of them piled into the elevator. There was always some drama in the elevator. Like this time there was a code white sign posted, which meant somebody had tried to slip out.

People were always escaping. You could get a day pass and not come back. One guy on their ward, José, had done that, and then had come back after four days. After three more weeks they gave him another pass and he went out and shot up and came back all nodded out. Then, they tossed him out. For refusing to take the test, Linda the night nurse told Lane. They would have let him stay if he had just fessed up. They would always take you back in the Motel. The Motel was the end of the line.

And J.D. tried to escape, the quick way, and that was why she wasn't coming to the *musicale*, because she wasn't allowed off the ward yet. And one guy, Lee, a tranquilizer addict had bribed a night guard, saying he was better, man, he was better, honest, and lit out for the Jersey shore.

Or you could go Against Medical Advice, which took three days and they'd let you out the front door. Invite you out. It was the upright escape, the calm way.

All this because the scary thing was to do your time and keep your mouth shut, and do what they told you.

The scary thing was to get better, to change. Because then they sent you back into the world. To try again.

Around the door to the garden there was an impressive show of force, all fourteen or fifteen of the nurses and orderlies standing around with their arms folded or shepherding in the lost causes from the other wings of the hospital. Lane's ward headed for the back.

The performer—one lone guy with an accordion— was what Lane had expected. Handlebar mustache, candy striper shirt and bellbottoms. He set up his sheet music on a flimsy aluminum stand. Lane passed the time watching faces, considering etiologies.

And then he recognized a face.

It was Tony Crick. Tony, Max's brother.

Strangest thing happened to Lane. He stood up. Just the reminder of home. He stood up and he was smiling, and shouting over the heads of the residents. Even the accordionist looked up, from where he was crouched over some sheet music.

Lane shouted his name.

Tony Crick looked out over the seats, surveyed the faces, but didn't seem all that surprised to see Lane. Which he wasn't. He was austere looking, Lane thought. He was reserved. He wore a beard, now, a sort of graduate school beard, and a pair of linen pants, a dress shirt. It was not Tony Crick the cross-dresser, the pederast. This was how a man looked when he had grown up inside the Motel, come of age in here, prepackaged, assembled from diverse sources.

But Tony smiled. He reached into the aisle, across Elena, reached out. Then he crossed over the two of them to sit in the empty seat.

Lane said, "I didn't put it all together."

Tony said he never expected to see anyone from town ever again, much less in here.

"You've been in a while," Lane said.

"Eleven months," Tony said. "Time is up, though. Gotta be gone by the end of next week."

"Me too," Lane said. "Out Monday."

The director of the Motel came to the mike then. He looked like somebody's Dad, Lane thought, with his cardigan sweater, his formulaic hesitations. Every nuance—his adjustment of the microphone stand, his straightening of his spectacles—had a studied solemnity. It was a pleasure to see them all there; it was a pleasure to introduce another in their series of musical performances. Music had an important therapeutic value. He sat down in the front row.

A wearying smile settled over the accordionist's face. He readied himself. "I got something to tell you," Tony leaned over. "My brother told me—"

The jocular, ragtime chords of some early love song commenced. Max's name set Lane off, and he went back to remembering, to thinking he was a dead man, to thinking things would turn out badly. He didn't hear anything.

Much of the staff repaired to the admitting room next to the lounge. The accordionist moved into a couple of union songs—the pleasures of company and brotherhood, fraternity, hearth, home, and work.

Lane thought about how a kid like Tony must feel in the Motel. They listened to him in group therapy, how girls never liked him, how no one ever talked to him, how they always called him a girl. An endless list of humiliations. How much talk did it take, how much reassurance, before someone like Tony felt like he'd had enough and was ready to go? How long until he had evened things out? What if he never did? What if he'd missed a chance to be made whole early on, and now it was gone?

"It's about that girl," Tony whispered.

Lane shook his head.

"That girl Alice—" Tony said.

Lane tried to concentrate on the accordionist.

"It's *really* wonderful to see you all here," he said. "A lot of you probably aren't familiar with many of these older American songs, but don't let that stop you. This is the music your parents and grandparents grew up on and they learned to *love* its simplicity and joy. So join in, if the spirit moves you! *Feel free* to clap along and sing!"

He rattled off some of the titles to come—the song about someone being in the kitchen with Dinah and a bunch of songs about trains—and then he went straight into a medley of springtime melodies. "After all it *is* spring, isn't it?" he cried above the opening chords. Elena was tapping her feet throughout.

Tony leaned over again but Lane waved him off.

What would J.D. have made of the whole thing? On Monday he would leave her behind. A dozen high-security locks would separate them when he got out. People got out and they came back in like tidal flotsam. There was no reason to think he would never see her again.

The accordionist was trying to get the residents to sing along now, and Tony and Lane slid lower in their chairs. Up and down the aisles, pumping a carney song out of his wheezing and exhausted accordion, the candy striper tried to brutalize them—people who were too drugged or preoccupied even to register that they were outside of their bedrooms—into the sing-along. Some people gave in. The teens, even the skinheads and punks, seemed to take a perverse interest in the accordionist. Suddenly the Motel was singing *con brio*, raising up its dead heart, belting it out.

"Shit," Lane said.

Tony nodded. Elena was way off the melody but happy nonetheless.

And then applause broke out. There were only eighty of them in the whole place—it didn't add up to much—but the accordionist took it as the highest kind of praise, bowing severally to each section of seats before replacing his instrument in its case.

The director came back to the mike and asked everyone to proceed to their wards in an orderly fashion. The staff emerged from the admitting room, arms folded.

Tony and Lane sat. Residents passed.

"So Alice—" Tony said.

"I don't know if I'm up to it," Lane said. "To be honest."

Tony touched him gently on the shoulder.

"I know. I heard. That's what it's all about, see? They were apologizing. Max is all bent out of shape. He's all fucked up. He's lost his job and everything. He told me when I saw you that I should tell you how they both want to say it. They're sorry or whatever—"

"Well, then why doesn't she fucking tell me—"

"Because they decided to leave you *alone*, get it? They don't want to bug you. They're scared as hell and full of regret. They didn't think it was this bad, you know?"

The last of the residents were filing out and Shirley, the head nurse from Lane's ward, was watching them.

"I don't know," Lane said. "Maybe you oughta stay out of it, Tony. Nobody says anything to anyone's face anymore."

They stood.

"But it's not like that," Tony said.

Shirley was hustling them out now. Closing the door to the lounge behind them. But out in front, by the admitting desk, they stopped.

"Fuck." Lane said.

Tony shook his head.

"Well then maybe I'm not gonna see you until we get out," Lane said. "You're not code white or anything—"

Shirley didn't say anything while they hugged. Tony headed off one way and Lane the other.

Dennis and Scarlett met on Saturday night, out at her apartment. They had planned to go into the city, to take Dennis' van, but something had gone wrong with it. The van was leaking a blue oil smoke from the tail pipe. Scarlett wanted to see some paintings in the city, old paintings, paintings of saints and guys who had bought their sainthood and rich people who could afford to have famous painters do their portraits, these Northern Renaissance paintings, allegories of the Seven Deadly Sins and the Cardinal Virtues. The Gates of Hell still stood in the museum, as though no one had recognized that Hell was actually located in parts of Trenton, or Elizabeth, or Chromium, or Nungessers, or Perth Amboy. They figured they would get there by five and catch the last hour, dine in the city, and drive back over the bridge after nightfall, into western obscurity.

But when the van broke down again, they decided to go to the movies in Montclair. They took the bus. There was a foreign film, a French movie about incest that Scarlett wanted to see.

Downtown Montclair looked like it had just been sandblasted. It was like a woman who wears too much hairspray. There were stores on the main street named Swank Drive-in Cleaners and Wooden Cask Wines and Spirits. In Montclair, the car dealers sold designer drugs. It belonged in Fairfield County.

Dennis loved the way Scarlett looked though. She was wearing a black dress, some kind of hippy thing that bunched and trailed with the breezes, and black tights and a black tee shirt, and even a shirt on top of that, though it was hotter than August and puddles stood in the streets.

After the movie, the audience scattered. Scarlett walked with an irritated purposefulness. They'd hated the movie. They didn't know where to go to eat. They paced up and down scorched white sidewalks. Something about the movie. They just walked until they stumbled on this Mexican place, the kind of Mexican place they have in the suburbs where a guy in a tuxedo is strolling around singing the same two or three Spanish songs over and over.

Scarlett was saying, "And don't think it's easy my not telling her. Don't think I like it. If I was staying—"

"I don't think it's easy," he said. "It's not like that at all."

And they ordered, and he was polite, and he didn't lay a glove on her. He wanted to have a date that wasn't full of drama and vacillation. Dennis had shaved off his soul patch for the evening, and he didn't even look that much like a plumber anymore.

They talked again about how she was leaving. He said he was sad she was leaving, and he said he wished they had done this sooner. He said it even though he didn't mean it the way it sounded—sort of greeting card. He was just sorry. Scarlett told him she just got feeling like she wanted to be back home. And Dennis could understand it, except that he was home already and things still weren't going right.

The food came and went. The night came and went. It was just another date. It was no big deal. Dennis paid, even though he was trying to save money. Scarlett put up a fight and then gave in.

And they went back out to the main drag in Montclair, where no one speeded, except maybe those suburban guys who drank too much and plowed their expensive European cars into telephone poles and trees. But these guys weren't out that Saturday night, and everything was calm and orderly. When they got on the bus, Dennis put his arm around Scarlett, and she let him and that was nice. They got off the bus several blocks from the exterminator's place—in front of the Pinnacle Coffee Shop. And then they parted. The biggest victories in the smallest things. Nothing else to report on this for the time being.

Evelyn Smail sat in the living room. She had moved the carpet that had been piled on the couch for a while so that she could sit there and make the calls she had to make, but she delayed. There was too much noise really. The neighborhood was too noisy. On the other hand, her house was like a tomb. Since Alice had moved out. The past was buried under this emptiness. There was noise in her head. Neglect accumulated. Evelyn drank.

She had spoken with the real estate agent that afternoon and was assured that, barring unforeseen market developments, barring further economic disasters, she would fetch a good price for the house. It would not be hard to sell. And she could move, with ease, into a small place in the city—a condominium—for a comparable price.

She needed to inform her exhusband of this arrangement. And to tell him that this would leave him alone in the Garden State with his daughter. It would be hard. The conversation and the departure.

She decided to call Ruthie Francis first.

From her end the line rang dimly. A funereal tolling. It rang at length before Ruthie's husband picked it up. With his stern, deep voice he agreed to go fetch his wife. There was no hint of the difficulties in the household. His voice manifested a perfectly stoic resolve.

And then Ruthie came on.

Evelyn put her feet up on a box full of old curtains.

"Just wanted to check in. Awfully quiet around here."

She explained about the real estate agent. She elaborated on his regional accent and the vulgarity of his phrasing. And then she remarked about the call she needed to make.

"Oh, well it's nice of you to call," Ruthie said.

Evelyn spoke about layouts of various apartments, about railroad styles and dining 1's and half-baths and roof rights, about bridge loans and capital gains. Some abbreviation was taking place, some displacement. But Evelyn couldn't yield just yet. She asked when Ruthie was going out to pick up her son, though she already knew.

"The family therapy session tomorrow," Ruthie said and her voice trailed off. "And then on Monday—"

"Do you need anything? Is there anything I can do?"

"No. No, we're just sitting down to eat here. It's just us, just Leonard and me. And then I guess we'll—"

Ruthie trailed off again. Another sigh.

"If there's more," Evelyn said, "just go ahead—"

"I don't need to talk, Evelyn. I'm all talked out. I'm tired. I'm exhausted. I just need to rest for a while."

"Oh, I—"

Evelyn let Ruthie go. They disengaged. And now she was ready. She dialed the numbers. The slithering white noise on the line cleared between bells.

The gap between that act of dialing and his voice shouting hello—it wasn't the talk that she feared. It was that gap. That Evelyn had to call him periodically did not alleviate the problem. It was only six months since then. Six months was not enough to feel better about it—one fiftieth of what came before. When Evelyn admitted the thought and admitted all the boredom and lethargy and rage—and it was just this that had sent her into the European performance automobile last month, with the intent to leave town for good—it made the sudden electrical miracle of her car seem so technologically appropriate. Another twenty-five years might pass before her faith in the world would be restored. It would be worth it.

All this she thought as the phone reached the decisive ring, the ring on which the machine would engage. Her teeth were clenched and she gripped the phone as if she might use it for actual physical combat.

The fourth ring passed. No voice came. Evelyn eagerly awaited the eighth, on which she felt certain she could hang up, but she put herself through a ninth and tenth, before letting herself.

Evelyn missed her daughter.

Then the phone rang.

She let it ring for a while.

She was not certain who she expected, but it was none of the obvious choices. She didn't remember Lane's voice was so nasal. Thin and without a trace of feeling. The voice of someone who spent time reading phone books or collecting weather statistics.

"Pleased to . . . make your aquaintance again," she said, "even under such . . . circumstances."

"Well—" he said "I—uh—I was just hoping maybe I could—uh—talk to Alice . . . uh, for a minute or so. Nothing—no emergency or—"

What? She was startled. She was crossing the room, to the window, where she stared out over the lawn. Where? But maybe just to look at a sliver of his house. A light on a garage way down the block. What he was coming back to.

"I guess you, uh, know where, I am and I can, uh—"

"Well," Evelyn said, "in fact, she has moved out. Just yesterday, in fact. She came for the last of her things, and now she's living downtown. I can give you that number if you like."

"That'd be great," he said, "if you don't mind."

"Mind?" Mrs. Smail said.

She searched for Scarlett's number on the pile of scrap paper by the phone.

"Are you sure—" Evelyn started.

Then neither of them said anything.

"What?" Lane came back.

"Oh, I'm, well, I'm just surprised," she said.

And nothing again for a moment.

"Well, I guess, I'm gonna give her a try," Lane said.

"I'm sure she'd be delighted," Mrs. Smail said.

And then he disconnected. It happened fast.

Evelyn cradled the phone as though it would have blistered her to hold it longer. Out the window: the lights of these last outposts.

*　*　*

Lane paced back and forth, up and back, on that long corridor in the Motel where the nurses could see you coming the whole way, and if you were troubled in your gait, if your head hung, if your heart was burdened they could make it out the whole way down the hall. They could have it in your file, that blue binder safely stowed behind the nurses desk, by the time you got there. Lane paced the corridor. He looked in J.D.'s room, and she .was sitting up in bed now, reading a book. He waved. He went by Eddie's room, and the room of the guy who came in strapped down a couple of days before.

And then he stopped at the nurse's station, where Linda was lining up small cups and filling them with the spectral variety of psychotropic medications. Liquids for people like Lane's roommate, who could not be trusted to take his pills and who therefore had to be *seen* swallowing.

Linda looked up, nodded, and then attended to her work.

"What are you doing?" she said.

"Phone calls," he said. "Difficult."

He was hanging around, hoping for encouragement.

The lineup for medication happened the way it always happened. The reluctant people were reluctant. People who were trying to lay off substances didn't like taking these other ones. But you never could tell. They liked it in secret, maybe. Lane liked taking his pills, which stabilized him, though they made him bleed from his asshole and have the driest, stickiest mouth he had ever had.

"No advice?" Lane said to Linda, as he swallowed the prescription.

"You're just about done with what we have to tell you," she said.

The line crowded in.

Everything quieted on the hall. It was a little after sundown. Lane had got ahold of Alice's mother on the phone—his heart was thundering, he felt like a marathon runner—and soon he had the number written on the yellow legal pad he had brought with him.

He dialed the number. It rang. Alice picked it up.

"Hi," he said. "This is Lane calling."

There was a fumbling on the other end, a gathering or regathering of forces.

"Well, hi."

"I, uh, I talked to, uh, Tony Crick this afternoon. And your name—well, he told me that you and Max . . . Well, I guess I wanted to set some things straight and all. I'm just feeling kinda bad about things, you know. You know where I am, right? 'Course you know."

Silence, then. Alice didn't say anything. Lane breathed. He was looking back and forth down the corridor. Then he just started talking. All these decisions came about as though they were made somewhere else, not in his own head. It was like taking dictation. He told her about where he was, about how there was this day the second week there when he had suddenly known he would survive, about how everything cleared in that moment. Like some long, involved fugue coming to its resolution. Lane told Alice about women. He told her his crimes—not even knowing if she was listening. He told her about the woman in his philosophy class in college. He told her about how there'd been another girl at the patent law firm. He had never said a word to either of them. He had spent so much time alone. He didn't know how many afternoons had passed this way. There was no way to start all the conversations he owed. He didn't even know where to begin. Books might be better than people. He told her how he was afraid of women and afraid of men too, and how he felt at the roof party, and how it felt when he fell, and how he had wanted to jump, and he told her about civic corruption and philosophical disenfranchisement and the hypocrisies of patent law. He told her about his lust for the outdoors. He told her everything that had gone wrong, everything he had lost, everyone who had hurt him, and then he told her about his father.

This went on for fifteen minutes. It was a torrent of language without much sense. Lane was aware of the words tumbling from his mouth and of the commotions in the hall around him, but he didn't pay attention to it. He just talked.

"So I don't know. I don't know," he said, stopping for breath. "I just wanted to tell you that. Let's not pretend we never met or anything. Let's talk when I get out, if you want, I mean. If you think it's okay."

Alice didn't get a word in, because by then the time limit on the call was up, and Linda was coming to flag him down.

Alice said, "Cool."

And Lane said, "I gotta go. You can't stay on—"

Goodbye.

7 / Another scorcher—from the window of the lounge where they were having cognitive therapy on Sunday morning, or maybe Lane was just making it up, knowing that his mother was probably here by now, that she was probably talking to his social worker, that the social worker was probably asking his mother questions about difficult pregnancies, drinking during childbirth, primal scenes, and child abuse. Just thinking it was a scorcher, because of remembering.

Hot, hot, hot. So Lane was having trouble concentrating on cognitive therapy which was dealing that day with anxiety. They were dealing, in fact, with some of Lane's fears, which he had enumerated while he waited to be summoned: conversation, nights with clouds, murder and murder with struggle, clocks, laughter, poetry, and technology. He was afraid of the elderly (and of becoming elderly), of Africa, of air-raids. He was afraid of the genetic pool and primogeniture and inheritance. He was afraid now of parties and of gods or the lack of them. He was afraid of pugilism.

Of liquor stores. He was afraid of Paterson, New Jersey. He was afraid of any kind of marital situation: married, unmarried, widowed, or divorced. He was afraid of any good day and the responsibilities implied therein and of what he might say and of what expressions others wore when he spoke with them on the telephone. He was afraid of what was to come and of getting out. And mostly he was afraid of his own life and opinions, of his past which came back to him in an incremental battle of inches.

What they did with Ed, the cognitive therapist—a decent likeable guy, but not one who could smell fear the way they, the residents, could—was to take somebody's routine fear and write it up on a chalkboard. J.D.'s fear of lamps, for example. Then they tried to name all the things that would go on in her mind as she approached, in this case, a lamp. Was J.D. afraid of turning on a lamp? Or turning one off? How did she feel about lampshades? Was she afraid of electromagnetic fields?

She sat by impassively through most of this, mumbling or not saying anything at all. But she wasn't going to sit still much longer, and any old manic depressive could tell. Her hands started to shake as Ed took up the issue of night lights. It was comic, but not to J.D. Lane had come to see that matters of life and death could lurk in the most routine appliances or activities. People could stake their very lives on the act of riding an elevator or going out for a newspaper.

J.D.'s hands were like fish flopping on the armrests of her chair. No one said anything. She looked like she was making it up, trying to get out of cognitive therapy, until she started convulsing. The nurses came in. The session lurched to a halt. They gave her a shot—she was offering her arm and whispering "No, no" at the same time—and then she was out cold. Slumped on the couch in the lounge. Ed calmly swept his eraser across the blackboard. They all filed out. No one spoke.

Every day he lost a friend, just for recovering. Only a couple of weeks ago, it seemed as though J.D. was really going to bounce back. Not now. He didn't even bother to learn the names of the new guys coming in.

Down the hall his mother was saying, probably, *it's not like he's telling you, it's not like he was always miserable, it's not that he couldn't get along with anyone.* But if not, how was it? His mother's wishes were as much wishes as his own. Which memory, twenty years later, did not retain the traces of wishful thinking? No assemblage of evidence, of snapshots, would help now. When the poison in his head vanished, he would come around. No revisionism was necessary.

Soon his social worker came through the locking doors at the end of the hall, with a set of keys the sizing of a hanging plant, and ushered him through, into the offices. In profile, his mother's face was nothing like her face two days before. There was trouble in her posture.

His social worker managed to get a red slash of lipstick across her face each day, but beyond this she always seemed threatened by the tasks she faced. Mountains of paper work were piled on her desk and on the various side tables in her office. She cleared a space for Lane.

He fell into the empty chair.

Ruthie clutched her purse firmly. Her skirt was carefully arranged over her knee. She greeted him quietly. He was the contestant emerging from the soundproof booth. The social worker brought him up to date about his past—he was neither well-liked nor unliked as a child, his parents' marriage had been neither cordial nor violent, he had done reasonably well at sports and reasonably well at his studies, and so on. These assessments had none of the garish colors he remembered, the brilliant moments of humiliation and degradation. It wasn't life as he had lived it.

His social worker spoke each sentence as though it was an elaborate gesture of respect. She said, "What doesn't matter of course is whether or not what Lane says about his past is true or not true."

Here the silence was sudden and unanticipated, and the social worker nodded at him, and he understood that he was supposed to say something now. He couldn't think of anything. A huge space widened between himself and any discussion of the past. He was supposed to absolve her, absolve his father, absolve his town, and he couldn't do it yet.

"Maybe we should start things off with a gesture of support on your part." She was talking to his mother now. "Maybe Lane would like it if you would tell him that you understand what these weeks have been like."

His mother now opened her purse.

She started to talk. She stopped.

"Oh dear," she said.

Ruthie leaned over to take his hand, then, and the purse slid off her lap, like a canoe going over a waterfall, and she didn't reach for it. He didn't want to take her hand—maybe Ruthie didn't know the rule forbidding physical contact, and he felt like setting her straight or like tipping over a pile of those cursorily alphabetized documents on the side table there. He didn't want to be touched.

In the meantime, the social worker was talking about love, about declarations of love like they were the easiest kind of talk, some little bit of language you could enter into like *may I please go down to the lounge and play chess with the guards*. He couldn't say these things. And after all this time of sitting in front of the television out in Haledon, and stealing booze and prescription drugs, hiding out, playing dumb words weren't going to bring him around instantly.

But there his mother had said it, and he heard.

The social worker asked him if he had heard. He nodded. He let his mother take his hand. Their eyes were averted.

After a while, he said, "I don't want to stay, but I don't want to go. I'm terrified."

The social worker asked if Ruthie had heard and she nodded. The social worker was like some sort of floodgate, some sort of damage control. She urged them on—repeating things he had said in group— stalling them at certain controversies. He nodded and Ruthie nodded, and it was all coming back now, every dark bit of shading, all the obscurity. He remembered this place down by the old railroad station where they used to swing on a piece of rope strung between two old maple trees, and how the shadow between these trees looked like a noose to him. He remembered killing a stray cat, drinking his own blood. He had lived all his life in the same town, always unknown on the first day of a new year, always certain he would be struck by an oncoming train.

And he remembered each bit of his father's memory failing.

After twenty minutes, the social worker called it quits. She said, "Here are the details of your son's aftercare." Documents were signed. Lane hated all those signatures. Files changed hands—files with little equations in them, files with statements about the flimsiness of his constitution. After he was gone, these files would languish in those blue halls, waiting to be reread.

Hot in Haledon, too, hot and humid, chromium green clouds and ozone and radon, trapped over the city. The fan spun ineffectually. Scarlett had a standby seat on a plane out of Newark on Wednesday. She wanted to travel before Memorial Day. She wanted to avoid the rush, the beginning of summer with its crime sprees. She wanted to be back in the midwest before then, back with her family.

But she wanted to make one more day trip before she left, a trip into the city. She was drinking and going back over what happened when she was there. It was so easy when she was younger to pick up and leave. It was too easy. Anyway, Dennis said he wanted to go to the city with her, that he loved to go there, that he wanted to go with her. Anyway, he didn't know why it had been so long. Instead of the foreign movie thing this time.

She was on her third drink—and it was only lunchtime—when Alice came back. Her feet clumped wearily, militantly up the stairs. Alice was wearing a torn denim skirt. Her hair was up in a scarf and she had a blouse on, a real blouse.

"Come on in," Scarlett said, "put your feet up. It's the hour of the social lubricant. I'm having one."

They were both embarrassed. Some days just came and went. They were mustering hope and courage, but it wasn't all there yet. Scarlett didn't like it necessarily. Alice sat on the couch. She fiddled with the dials on the television, but the picture would not come in. They didn't talk about the call from Lane the night before. Not much came up between Alice and Scarlett lately.

"My dad's coming over," Alice said. "We're going out for this important luncheon. I don't know if he's gonna try and cut me off or something. Or what. Seems like it's some kind of big news. But he's coming soon. If you want to make yourself scarce, go ahead and get in the shower or go take a nap or something."

From the counter, Scarlett brought Alice her martini.

"I wouldn't mind meeting him, you know—"

"He looks like all the rest of them," Alice said. "All dads look the same. They have a certain kind of talk. You say 'but, Dad, last week you said . . .' That's my idea of a dad. My dad likes prime numbers and irrational numbers. All kinds of numbers."

"My dad is an accountant."

"Just what I mean," Alice said, "same exact thing."

They drank for a while. The apartment was in disarray. Same coffee cups in the sink day after day. They rinsed them out and used them over. Things going bad in the refrigerator. Health foods going bad.

"So what's he like?" Scarlett said.

"Who—"

"Your dad."

The buzzer sounded.

"He's gonna give me the same old rap," Alice said.

"Why don't you hide out?" Scarlett said.

"It's not worth it," Alice said. "Ever read *Home Renovator*? He's like that." She lifted the screen and flung the keys out. "He's got home renovator of the soul."

Scarlett turned off the television set. She went into her bedroom and lay down. Then, because she and Alice were in that part of roommateship, of friendship even, when mutual disappointment was a must, she waited for the front door to open, for the preliminaries to take place, and then she went back out, pretending she'd forgotten something.

He was small and very round. He was maybe five feet five. And he was fat. Couldn't miss it. He wore dark glasses; his shirt was open just one more button at the collar than any dad's shirt should be open; his chest hair emanated from the open space like some prolific weed.

"Oh," Alice said, "Dad, this is Scarlett."

"So pleased," he said, hand thrust out.

Then they stood there, awkward as they could be, conscious that some small thing none of them wished to learn had just been learned. The fan in the window went around and around and it was hot.

Lane got out.

People were sad to see him go, or they said they were. The Motel was a grand experience in abandonment or birth trauma. But like Lane had seen Elena go a few days before, back to the house where her mother had died, he had to go too.

The Garden State had grown while he was gone. It was big sky country now, a vast open expanse, a cut-rate warehouse of vistas. When he looked up at the sky, from the parking lot of the Motel, Lane was like an ancient astrologist. He examined his mother's luxury sedan, ran his hands across its chrome details, tried the door as though he was the first ever to have done so.

He could dance if he wanted.

May had so many colors. He'd forgotten all about it. And there were breezes, and the smell of freshly cut grass. He flipped around the radio and caught part of a baseball game and an opera and some born-again talk radio. There was rock and roll, although it was all this power ballad shit, and there was hip hop, and Lane smelled high octane fuel and plastics. In the orderly town of Bernardsville, he saw kids chasing an ice cream truck up a long slow incline. The rush of velocity was better than being born again.

The cast came off his wrist on Friday.

What was he going to do the rest of the day? It was only noon.

His mother said: "Do whatever you want. Why don't you just relax? Why don't you watch some television or work in the garden or something?"

The Garden?

"It needs your help."

Lane's stepgrandfather was coming to stay with them. His stepfather's father. Lane agreed to be, if possible, a decent host. His wife had just been hospitalized for, it seemed, the last time.

"I'm going to have to try to relax," Lane said. "I'm going to try to take it easy."

They moved onto Interstate Eighty, through the vaporous *sfumato* of its desolate expanses, under overpasses, alongside the hulking remains of empty factories. Gigantic cattails everywhere. They were taking the long way around.

"Maybe you should concentrate on one thing now—"

"I'll do whatever I want, thanks."

Ruthie laughed nervously.

"I will try to listen when you talk to me," he said. "I will try to get a new job. I will try."

"Lane—

"Look," he said, and he was facing her, seeing her

eyes, their color, the circles under them. He didn't know why he was so angry anyway. No reason in the world why these conversations couldn't go easier.

"My father—"

"Next week," Ruthie said.

"This week," Lane said.

"Lane—"

He shuddered.

"Next week," Ruthie said.

They were both tired already.

On Monday afternoon, Evelyn Smail drove in her loaner car into the city to meet with a real estate agent—a friend of a friend—to discuss one bedroom cooperative apartments. Sunny and hot: the highway was crowded in both directions. The car they loaned her at the dealership was a domestic model with plastic seats and neither radio nor air conditioning. As a perk, however, the dealer had thrown in a cellular telephone. He was trying to avoid being named in Evelyn's upcoming legal action.

She no longer trusted cars, though she was trying to shake off all ghosts of the past. Chief among the cardinal virtues, Evelyn thought, was hope, and on Monday she had hope in excess. She was driving. She was tangled up at a cloverleaf on the way to the bridge. She didn't see the gray van that streaked past her in the breakdown lane.

The tape player in Dennis' van was still broken, but he had brought along a portable one. He and Scarlett had it turned up enough that they didn't have to say too much. But that didn't mean he didn't still have to think.

Scarlett was talking about the city again, about graffiti artists and performance artists and a guy she knew who had been a painter and now lived on the street. Once when she passed him as he idled, arms outstretched, in some small square, he hissed at her— *I'm Halloween and I have nine lives!*—and the remark had stuck with her ever since. The street, someone had told her, was where you went to live when you no longer felt comfortable anywhere else. It was a system of thought as well as a circumstance.

Then she and Dennis argued about whether most bands were better before or after their records deals. Who could say? Who had these arguments anymore? The days were gone when being in a bar band was a state of grace. The days without moral consequences and without wasted lives were all gone now, and Dennis and Scarlett were remembering. When the tape came to an end and the conversation came to an end, there was a long silence, and Scarlett sighed and they both realized how bad the traffic was. They were in Fort Lee, now, a town organized around toll booths.

"Listen," Dennis said, coming out of a long dream, "we could just, like, cruise out on the Palisades Parkway and pull into one of the rest areas, and like just take a look for a while. Take it in."

Scarlett thought about it.

It was the afternoon now, and orange and red and ochre were reflected on the dusty gray buildings on the far side of the water. Their reflections danced amid the rippling confluence of fresh water and sea water.

"Otherwise, like a half hour here—"

"Yeah, all right."

Dennis swooped off to the right, gunning the van. Rusty old parts scraped and rattled inside. He ran a couple of red lights, just to remember. Horns sounded. They passed Kenny's Original Seafoods and Squitieri's

Funeral Parlour, which was maybe where they took that one guy from Paterson after he plunged off the Palisades, and they turned up a new tape and everything felt pretty good to Dennis and Scarlett. Green and green and more green. Country music and banjo instrumentals and Gospel and stuff: Scarlett had taped it off some late-night show out in the midwest.

"I really wish you weren't leaving." He started up all over again.

"Yeah," she said. She was looking out the window. "Well, I could always come back. It might only be for like two weeks or something. I mean, how long can you live with your family anyway? It can't last too long."

"Sure," Dennis said, and then he leaned over to kiss her. He was driving and leaning over, and Scarlett wanted to be kissed, certainly, and so she closed her eyes and their lips met, and Dennis lost track of the van for a second and he had to swerve to avoid running over the rear end of a little subcompact ahead of them.

"Settle down," Scarlett said. "Better find the Rest Area. The scenic vista."

It wasn't too far. Maybe five miles. They were heading for the northern border of the state and the landscape was luminous now. Easily as good as in any of the paintings they might have seen, those representations of light that were not light itself.

The Rest Area was empty, and the van had barely rolled to a stop before they began again. Gentle kisses, nothing carnivorous. Kisses which did much, now, to purge regret.

"Shit," Scarlett said under her breath.

They kissed for a while, and then Dennis put his hand on her breast. They were back at the origin of kissing, of being in love, of being in a van doing it, and they were working their way forward in time. She was wearing this torn tee shirt under a black cardigan sweater and he crept under the layers like he was throwing off a legacy.

Then they got down out of the van and bushwacked into the woods. He had this thought that there would be pines and pine needles. Beds of pine needles. But the way down the hill to the edge of the cliffs was marred by undergrowths of poison ivy and skunk cabbage and beer bottles. Weed trees everywhere.

But then they got up on some rough outcropping there, and you could see the whole fucking megalopolis over there. That river was bigger than any city, bigger than any temporary riverside development. Dennis felt how rivers commanded so much myth, so many stories. It was the kind of expanse that could not help but be dignified. And then there was the north end of that island. The color of slate, the color of tombstones. So much activity, none of it visible from that distance. So much disappointment. That's what Scarlett said. Its spires were jagged insistences; its churches subscribed to alchemical philosophies, heretical rituals. Its universities protected abandoned, discredited theories, like the theory of the flat earth, the theory of the earth-centered universe, and the Pleasure Principle. They were glad to be on this side.

Dennis encircled Scarlett with his arms. They lay down on the rocks. Graffiti, like ancient texts, was scrawled across its surfaces. They kissed some more and it didn't matter that it was hot again—the hottest May on record—and there was ozone trapped over the metro area. The sun sank back over Paramus, over the mall. Schoolkids were out for the summer and they were coming this way, to drink, to plunge off the rock, just like generations past. Dennis knew their every step.

All silent in the dining room there, the comforting shuffle of his mother's steps as she headed back into the kitchen to get the vegetables (green beans), the baked potatoes. His stepfather said nothing, pausing at his own task: carving (pot roast), to drink from a tumbler of Scotch (neat). The lights were low (rheostat), the potatoes microwaved, the atmosphere a little tense.

Lane quietly turned the crystal stem at the right corner of his table-setting upside-down. And then he headed back into the kitchen himself, looking for a glass to fill with milk. When he was younger he used to go out into the kitchen to avoid conversation. In those moments the clean, empty array of modern technologies, the shining aluminum and copper and iron and stainless steel and silver, pleased him.

"Where's Dennis?"

Ruthie held the last potato in her gloved hand and carried it across the kitchen to a serving plate where three others waited.

"In the city," she said.

"When's he moving his stuff?"

"What difference does it make?"

"Who's he in the city with?" Lane said. He stared into the recesses of the refrigerator filled now with health drinks and lowfat diet plates and jars of multi- and megavitamins—heavy metals in small doses, lecithin, yogurt cultures.

"With Scarlett, you know the—"

Ruthie betrayed no opinion. Lane remembered

about being up on the roof, just before the blackout. He poured milk into an old glass. The two of them went back into the dining room. His stepfather—in a beige linen jacket—was adjusting his spectacles, the better to serve the strips of roast onto the plates gathered around the serving platter. Ruthie and Lane sat, and the potatoes went around, and the green beans, and the colors were comforting to Lane. The steam rising from the microwaved potatoes was comforting. He made do with the condiments at hand and everything seemed fine.

He hoped he would not hurt his family in the future.

His stepfather hoisted up his glass: "Welcome back."

And Ruthie raised her glass too. Lane couldn't figure out if it was the right thing to do—suffer through a toast—but he just smiled anyway. They started to eat.

Ruthie said, "Your grandfather is going to sleep in Dennis's bedroom by himself. If Dennis stays the night, he's going to sleep in the library on the couch."

Lane nodded.

They ate.

"Your grandmother is quite sick now," she went on. "If you can talk to him, you know, he would be very grateful."

"He remembers you, you know," his stepfather said. "In fact, Mother remembers you too."

Ruthie refilled her wine glass, and soon his stepfather disappeared into the pantry. The music of bottles colliding. Lane imagined Scotch being levied with a compulsive exactitude.

"What are Dennis and Scarlett doing in the city?" Lane asked.

"Museum," Ruthie said.

Lane said, "I don't know—"

His stepfather stood in the doorway, looked in, and then, retreated back into the kitchen.

"I know, dear," Ruthie said. Exhaustion was etched in small crosshatchings around her eyes and mouth. "It's going to be hard."

"I don't think you want to hear it," he said. "You don't want to hear what I have to say."

"That's just not true."

He took up his silver again. Inarticulated by remorse. He flung his things down on the plate, and remnants of dinner scattered out around him. Because you checked yourself into the Motel, you got out, you took your medication, and still you had only made the smallest dent.

"Shit," Lane said, "fucking shit."

"What?" Ruthie said.

His stepfather came back in, tentatively, with more rolls.

"I don't know how I'm going to work."

Everything was so tense.

"I want to go into the city," Lane said. "Maybe I can get Dennis to drive me into the city tomorrow."

"It's Tuesday tomorrow," Ruthie said. "Other people are on a work schedule."

"I know what fucking day it is," Lane said.

"Calm down," his stepfather said.

And then silence.

Then, suddenly, everyone was getting up. Lane was getting up, too. All in agreement not to talk about it anymore, for now. Part of the mute world. He knew it. Already the Motel was becoming something that existed only in his memory, with no analog in Short Hills, or an analog only dimly evident now, across this great expanse of space and time.

*   *   *

After dark on Monday when Max Crick came to in Bayonne, at the edge of the Newark Bay. It smelled like chemical warfare out there, like slow death. His brother had called him from Short Hills. Getting out, coming home, at last. Where was home, though? Good thing he called, because Max's phone was dead to all but incoming calls now, and it looked like he was going to have to get rid of the trailer and move back into town. He was having trouble with payments, with lots of kinds of payments. And Giolas had volunteered to let him sleep on the couch at his place and Nails Penne-baker would let him sleep at his place, and maybe Lane would let him sleep on the couch over there, since Dennis was moving out anyway. Until something opened up.

How was Nails holding up, was one thing he wanted to know. Working in the car wash? So much bitterness in the world. So many fucked-up jobs. How did anyone hold up? He didn't think Tony would be able to, outside of the place in Short Hills, and neither could Lane, for example. Max had certain resources, though.

Which had all brought him back to thinking about Mike Maas. It wasn't too far from Bayonne that Mike did what he did. You could talk a thing to death trying to figure out how it happened. Tony even remembered playing with matches with the guy one time. Tony said Mike was obsessed with fire, but no more so than anyone else. We all love to watch things consumed by fire. It was like television, Tony had said, you could just stare and stare into it.

Mike didn't have any secret life, though. Not that anyone could tell. He didn't gamble away his mother's house or anything. Unless he took the secret life down with him. No, too easy an explanation. Tony didn't set himself on fire. Lane didn't. Nails Pennebaker didn't set himself on fire either, or push his kid off a building or shoot his wife, and he had plenty of reasons.

There wasn't much to remember of Mike now, anyway, except how he died. The memories were themselves of memories, descriptions for the sake of sensation. Only Mrs. Maas remembered. And Max. Max's problem was not being properly able to forget. Mrs. Maas had told him *Michael was a top student, a top singer in the school chorus, a top athlete.* None of these things was really true, but Max didn't say anything—that time he visited. He let her talk for a while. He thought about a time when his mom wasn't dead, a time which didn't exist in his memory, but which he could imagine.

He told Mrs. Maas how much he missed Mike and how he wished all that hadn't happened. It wasn't much, but he had come out of his way to say it, and he didn't care now if it was awkward to bring it up after all this time. The town was to blame, the state was to blame, the era, genetics. Mike was to blame. He could have held on.

Now he was out on the piers looking over the goddamn Newark Bay thinking how beautiful were the lights of all those factory spaces.

He had promised to meet L.G. at midnight at Dover's and he was over forty-five minutes from town now, and that was just if the traffic went right. On the other hand, he had his scooter back now, and he could just blow off the whole thing and cruise the tunnel. That way, there were panoramas of the state. Industrial cranes on all sides dwarfed those waterways like the wading birds of prehistory. Barges came and went.

Max finished the last beer in the sixpack, and heaved the empties into the bay. It was late. He was here way beyond any reasonable expectation. So much peace now. So much to look forward to.

The nicest part of the last couple days in Haledon was when Scarlett went home after fucking around with Dennis in Palisades Park. It was late. She didn't even know how late it was. The sun almost never set in May, but it was gone now. Scarlett came in tiptoeing, the taste of him still in her mouth, bits of foliage clinging to her, traces of poison ivy here and there, to find Alice asleep on the couch just a denim jacket covering her. Not wearing too much, wearing just some lingerie. So much like a kid in sleep that you'd never believe she was an adult.

Alice didn't snore. She was as still as if deceased. What made slumberers unique, Scarlett realized, was that they have no choice but to trust. No way around it. Therefore, when you prepare for bed, make sure your affairs are in order.

Scarlett wanted to kiss Alice, to take advantage of her in that way, to testify a little to that thing near to love that roommates never realize they have until they're living with the next detestable partner. She didn't. Instead, she took off her shoes in the doorway, set them by the pile of shoes—some of them Alice's, some of them her own, not yet packed—and wriggled out of her green tights and her cardigan sweater and left these in a clump.

In the kitchen, she decided to have tea. She filled the stained stainless steel kettle with bottled water, and then she wept silently, for a second, about having met Alice's boyfriend and liking him and taking off and leaving him and Alice behind, both sleeping on couches in various parts of town.

The phone rang.

She checked the clock as she was tripping over an ashtray on the floor, running to catch the phone so that it wouldn't wake Alice, running so the machine wouldn't go off—she was breathless and irritable, as she unholstered that beige plastic fist.

Then she gave up all pretense of quiet, and shook Alice until she woke—Alice mumbling *fuck shit fucking shit oh fuuuuck*, until upright. Then Scarlett went into her bedroom to await the wailing kettle.

"What's going on—" Lane said.

"What do you mean, what's going on?" Alice said. "I just woke up. I'm sitting on the couch here where I was sleeping. It's like, I don't know. It's like early morning and I have to go on a job interview tomorrow."

"What's the interview?"

"It's in the mall. I'm gonna try and sell leather goods."

"Leather goods—" Lane said.

"Hey, well—"

Lane went on. "Well, if you're going on a job interview in the morning, maybe we should just, I don't know. Because, I don't know, I had this idea. I'm like thinking of going into the—"

"Hang on a second," Alice said. "Because I'm—"

"Yeah, I might want to go into the city," Lane said, "for the morning and I thought you might want to go or something. I don't know. I want to go and look around. See my old apartment. I just want to go back there. I thought we could drive in or something. In the morning, for a while."

"What's—do you have a car?"

"No, I—"

"—have to catch a bus or something," Alice said. "I have a schedule around here or maybe Scarlett does.

"Scarlett where's the fucking—"

She muted the thing.

She came back on the line a little too fast.

"Are you sure?" Alice said.

"I didn't tell my mother," he said, "you know what I mean? But it's not anything. It's just going into the . . . I'll get to the shrink and everything. I'll tell everyone everything. I'm just going into the city to—"

"I'd love to," Alice said.

"Everyone says I'm not supposed to go and see my father and okay I get the picture, but—"

"You're not missing much," Alice said.

Then there was a long silence. Lane sighed.

Alice said, "When are we meeting?"

Lane said, "Let's go early. Let's catch like a ten o'clock bus or something."

And that was it. After that, Alice couldn't sleep. She had plans.

No one had turned out liked they guessed, but no one had turned out half bad, if the trick to being okay in that decade was being reasonably straightforward and not coveting anyone else's property or station. That second-to-last night with Scarlett they stayed up for a long time and watched late night television and talked about everything—how flat this country is, whether religion will make a late comeback, whether Lane slipped or jumped when he fell onto the fire escape, what made Mike Maas do it, how long until the recession, whether rock and roll was really dead.

* * *

Resolution is ephemeral. You're more likely to win Lotto than to experience revelation. Get yourself in order for revelation, nonetheless. What Haledon liked was three-day weekends. In the middle of a week in May its citizens were planning ways of escape, ways of getting to the shore. That May was so hot that the shore was the last refuge, though there was all that worry about what was going to wash up.

Elsewhere, too, the long weekend eclipsed the tidal movements of Americans to hometowns, out of hometowns, out across the land, some restless exodus with no particular destination. It eclipsed the movement of those who were leaving the East, going to places like Austin, Tallahassee, Baton Rouge, Cheyenne—not exactly nowhere, but not the kind of places we expect people to leave here for. Thoughts about the weekend eclipsed the subtle activity of growing old and growing shrewd, that incremental willingness to compromise.

The long weekend, and the inevitable gatherings of family and friends—parties at the shore, dinners at the air-conditioned restaurants on Haledon Avenue—these didn't ameliorate, even as they concealed, the real problems. Maybe language couldn't even speak to tell what troubled us, though the torrents of language—discussions of chance and probability, decline and fall—always blasted away at the silences somehow. The sound of trains, for example. That's why the sound of guns on Memorial Day—those salutes to soldiers lost in wars most people don't remember—are so moving, and why the rhythm of drill sergeants is like hip-hop and why rock and roll sounds medieval sometimes and why all the great plots are used up and why everyone at the parade feels they have lost something.

Lane searched around his house for a round trip

ticket. He thought there was a commuter ticket around and that he wouldn't have to pay. But Ruthie loaned him the three dollars at last, without comment, and it bothered him somehow. He wanted no handouts.

He shaved, and he put on black jeans and a tee shirt—even though he had to steal them from what was left in Dennis's dresser—and he paced around the house for a while, making peace with things. Then he swallowed some antidepressants with his coffee and he was ready.

Meantime, at the mall, L.G. was talking to the higher-ups at the L.T.D. Carpet Company about a guy he knew who had done some retail sales stuff who might really be good as a floor salesman. For days, L.G. had fretted over the wording of this act, but when it came down to it, it wasn't the wording that bothered him. It was whether or not to make the pitch. Still, the higher-ups were willing to see this guy, this Max Crick. It didn't seem to jeopardize the negotiations involved in L.G.'s hiring. Because, for the moment, L.G. was the carpet salesman's carpet salesman, a guy who could sell unwoven straw to a rich lad and praise its Asian charm. He breathed a sigh of relief and got ready to head out on the floor, for one of his last days here at the Paterson outlet. After shooting the breeze with the guys in the office, he forgot all about Max for a while, about moving to Paramus Park. He was think-ing, instead, about words, and how with the right ones white was black and American cars ruled the roads.

And Max was at his father's place which was not too far from the bus stop where Lane was waiting. Suddenly he hadn't wanted to be alone in the trailer anymore. It was such a bad feeling that he had decided he was willing to be with his father. He was willing. And as he sat awake on Wednesday morning, thinking *this is the day Tony comes back*, he imagined his father asleep in the next room dreaming dreams of filicide—his father happily strangling him or forcing him to stick his hand in a toaster. Maybe with Tony looking on.

Max had visited Nails last night, at his place in Paterson, but Nails wasn't there. As his wife explained (kid lurking in the background, lost expression on his face), Nails was residing in a therapeutic community. Some kind of rehab thing that lasted *two years*. What would the kid know of him when he got out of there? What would his wife remember about him?

And Dennis had got up early, thinking about Scarlett. He'd slept in the van again, and now he was parked by the train station, drinking a quart of orange juice that he just grabbed out of the refrigerator during a quick stop at his father's house. He was thinking he wished she'd just get on the fucking plane already and buckle herself in. And he was wondering what he would do tomorrow.

And he thought about what happened on the roof, and that moment when he thought that Alice had pressured Lane up there. And he thought about going down the fire escape and picking Lane up where he was passed out with his arm all bent around like he was some puppet that had just been cut loose from its strings. Lane all passed out. Trying to wake up, and thinking of him then as *brother, brother*, close to death, picking him up, dusting him off, persuading him to go back up the ladder and face all those people who were peering over the ledge, face all that silence, all those people trying to figure things out. All those people attributing causes and effects as fast as possible. Remembering all that. Wondering if you could ever relate again to someone you had seen in those circumstances. Wondering, and wanting to talk to Lane like they used to talk sometimes, like people who are not related still giving a shit anyway. Wanting to talk about anything, about what Lane was thinking about, whatever he thought about things, wanting Lane to tell him stuff, teach him a few things. Tell him about painting. Wanting to give Lane a piece of his mind. Liking the guy and hating the guy. Wondering, and hoping.

And Scarlett was wearing overalls, these same overalls she wore as a kid, and she was going down the stairs of the building, past the exterminator—who was wearing a sleeveless tee shirt because it was supposed to be in the nineties that day, and humid—and onto the street, empty now because the rush was over and people were settled in for another day. It was going to be nice to be home again, and to have her mother complain about her dyed hair, and to watch empty stretches of road where nobody bothered to go anymore. To see snakes and guys decked out in fishing gear. It was going to be nice to get one thing back, even if you had to lose some other stuff to do it.

Ruthie Francis, on her way up the street to the Smail residence, took in the humidity of Wednesday absently. She felt a little noise in her skull, a hopelessness about her children, her sons, her marriage. She felt envy about Evelyn Smail's decision to leave town. What was left here now, anyway, a new generation of professional couples who had overpayed for their half-acre lots, with their spoiled attitudes, bedroom community values? What would happen to her son, and how could she avoid feeling responsible for it? What had happened to her, since her youth?

The street was still—small groups of boys playing at the ends of driveways, silently excavating bits of earth from lawns and around shrubs—but Ruthie was certain now that dread lingered in each of these houses, little pockets of dread and uncertainty.

But Evelyn Smail, waiting for Ruthie, was unnaturally happy. It had nothing to do with anything, really, not to do with the sound of a train passing, with the ample sunshine, with the hummingbirds on the feeder in the backyard, or with the fact that she was packing the last of these things for a likely departure within the next month, by, say, the first official day of summer, but just *because*. It was the same feeling she had had that day, when merely out for a spin up into the hills, she had realized that any moment she might just keep going. But the sentiment had deepened. Evelyn climbed the stairs to what had been her daughter's room, and she danced a dance there along the empty floorboards. She had lost everything.

Alice Smail of the strong opinions saw Lane at the corner, wearing, well wearing too much black, really. He looked as good as she would have guessed. Everything was possible. Public education could be possible in a world like this one, ethnic coexistence and regional harmony. Whatever agency caused Lane to change his mind and call her, whatever patron saint of small apologies and forgivenesses, she was indebted to it.

The hug was short, and the bus came soon after it. Lane tried to keep his body several inches away while he hugged, but she was close enough to smell his hair and to take in the color of his eyes and to see that they were a little bloodshot. Then the bus came. They submitted several dollars in change. They went straight to the back.

Lane and Alice talked about bus rides they had taken, times they had been in the city, how the fares had gone up over the years, how the buses were nicer than they used to be, the best routes into the city, and late night drives across the county when they were younger, and how dangerous the roads were late at night, and people who had driven off the bridge, and people they knew who were dead, and then, avoiding names of people they knew well, they talked about drinking.

After that, there was a long silence.

It was a conversation like that old handkerchief trick. The more they said, the more there was to say, but none of it did anything, none of it made either of them feel that they were understood, that human companionship could quench the intensity of loneliness. The conversation was like so much pavement under the wheels of the bus. It was like landscapes crisscrossed a thousand times but unknown, except by billboards. Still, it was worth it.

The bus passed through terrain urban and industrial and then densely urban. There were factories on either side, oil tanks, cranes, stacks billowing flame and smoke, parking lots full of foreign cars. Not a soul to be seen anywhere.

That week in the western part of the state, a man had opened a radiotherapy device and pronounced its glowing contents to be religious artifacts. That week in New Jersey, a man had dive-bombed his private plane into a football stadium during a track and field contest. That week bookies in Atlantic City had taken bets on the likely crash point of a government satellite. Nothing was a prise anymore, Lane argued, except human kindness.

They came out of the wasteland by the bridge. The

view from the Jersey side was beautiful that morning. Green and gray and activity everywhere. On the bus there were children who could not sit still, who couldn't tell one state from another, who didn't know about the Jersey Devil or other local hauntings. There were elderly people, people who ought to have been at work earlier, but were not. Up into the mountains, down to the harbor, that vast river. When the bus came down from the bridge, onto the cloverleaf, it circled around and around a rubble of shattered glass and abandoned automobiles. City of narcolepsy, city of machinations, city of public executions and prerecorded accompaniments and prenuptial agreements, city of basis points and in vitro fertilizations and squatter's rights and electroconvulsive therapy and dreamlessness and aberrations of need. The bus took a right turn at the university and headed down along the river.

Lane's past crowded him. Not just his movements along these streets, past the bodegas and delicatessens that lined them, but the place and its spirit. He didn't feel like he was back or like he was home. He felt like part of him had vanished. But he knew that he had always felt that way. Part of him had always vanished. It didn't seem so bad. He was so excited by topography that he grabbed Alice by the blouse at one point, as they passed the unfinished cathedral uptown. He held her for a moment.

And then they were going through one of the old drug locations where guys Lane had known at the firm had gone to cop substances for professional all-nighters. And then they were in midtown, threading their way through the static crowds and traffic. They went around and around another cloverleaf, behind a long caravan of buses that had come from Peapack, Blunt, Tyre, Mahwah, Summit, Ho Ho Kus, and Teaneck, and then the bus roared in among the others, coughing and sputtering, and disgorged them.

Even the stairwell was crowded with bodies. That was the first thing. They lay sleeping head to foot at the top of the silently scrolling escalator, and the commuters each picked their way through that gauntlet of bodies. Lane and Alice did, too, wary of trampling an ankle or a hand stretched out casually across the floor. There were four guys sleeping at the top of the stairs, but they didn't look like vagrants. They had the right sneakers, expensive basketball sneakers. They were American and the place was air-conditioned and this was where they lived.

It was a maze of nests and habitations. The stairs opened out onto a newsstand, and on either side of it were the billiards room and the betting parlor. Emaciated shades stood by O.T.B. with carefully folded newspapers, checking and rechecking the figures. They scanned the passers-by and then returned to their work. Nobody moved. The bettors took a step this way or that—interrupting the transient populations with questions or needs—and then they rested again. Confidence games abounded, games about credibility. Panhandling was the career of last resort, but the language that characterized it was as precise as legal language and as persuasive as a public relations campaign.

There was a gigantic sculpture in one wing of the building, a haphazard array of wires and fixtures, through which the same five balls—duckpin bowling balls—rolled, day after day. The transients marveled at the sculpture. The residents detested its regularity.

There were fast food establishments where no one ate because the homesteaders inside had appropriated each and every booth. With their belongings strewn around them, they were busy in the act of enumeration. There were policemen and women on the beat; there were transvestites on their way up Eighth Avenue; there were lovers in the men's room, and dealers behind every pillar. The Terminal was where Lane and Alice had ended up, and it was where you ended on any of several different journeys.

They stood for a minute at one of the newsstands, surrounded by hardcore pornography.

"We made it," Lane said.

"Sure did."

"I thought you—" he said. "I was thinking it was going to be so weird to come back. I didn't even think—"

"I haven't been here in a while," Alice said.

"But it was nice of you," Lane said.

"I almost feel like getting out of town again."

"Thanks," Lane said. "Wait."

They walked down by the glass doors, which opened by themselves when Alice stepped into the purview of a camera mounted there. There was a blast of tropical air. People rushed in around them.

And Lane left off thinking about the past right then, when the doors opened.

"Alice," he said.

With all that in front of them, they looked up.